HEATHER BOYD

Just a Dream

HUNT CLUB – 4

DEDICATION

Many thanks to my wonderful editor Sandra Sookoo
for her words of advice and patience.

By Heather Boyd

Almost an Equal
Barely a Master
Hardly a Stranger

Just a Dream
Never a Gentleman
Once a Husband

CHAPTER ONE

March, 1815

"And what are your thoughts, Lord Raphael?"

Rafe, suddenly aware that all eyes in the Hunt Club's smallest dining room had turned in his direction, quickly lifted the cigar to his nose and drew in a deep breath of the scent as expected. Cigars and port usually required less consideration, but the club's oldest member, the Duke of Staines, was in an odd mood today and seemed to require his participation in every discussion.

He released his breath slowly, and met the duke's sharp gaze. Then he shrugged. "I'm sorry, Your Grace, but I have no strong opinion on the subject."

There were few at the club tonight, most patrons committed to attend social events at less exclusive venues than this. Rafe didn't exactly wish he were at one of them suffering mashed toes and polite conversations with chits he had no interest in but hoped the duke might find some other source of amusement soon.

The duke sniffed the cigar he held and then passed it to his ever-present shadow, a footman named Redding. "I think three dozen for the bedchambers. I'm sure a few of the members could be enticed to appreciate them."

"Of course, Your Grace," Mr. Redding murmured as he returned the cigar to the box, tucked it under his arm, and excused himself from the room. The other guests added their agreement and filed from the room, likely intent on discovering a quiet corner or a rowdy bedchamber to frolic in with a tempting bed partner. Rafe stood too, intent on the former for what remained of the night.

The duke returned his attention to Rafe and prevented his escape. "Now tell me, what can I do to make you happy, Lord Raphael, since the problem is neither the standard of the cigars nor the port? You've been a member for a few years and you still seem ill at ease. Does the club lack an entertainment you require? You've only to ask and we shall be happy to provide whatever you need."

Under the intense scrutiny of the older man, a flush of discomfort stirred in him. Even after a yearlong absence, there was little that went on in the club without His Grace hearing about it. Rafe had never expressed a single unhappy word from the moment of his induction. Few gained admittance to the club and friends often quizzed him as to why the club was so select in its membership. He couldn't say the real reason, but the club's diverse membership did make for exciting conversation. Patron's were quite varied, neither exclusively Whig nor Tory, young or old, lord or gentleman of wealth, sedate in their habits or prone to bring scandal wherever they went.

He was baffled by how he had come to His Grace's attention in the first place, but he wasn't planning to give up his membership. "The club is everything I dreamed and more."

A frown grew on His Grace's brow as he pulled out his pocket watch and checked the time. After a long moment, he snapped it closed and the frown disappeared. "The club exists to entertain and delight. Forgive me for pointing out that you neither appear entertained or delighted on most occasions."

Rafe smiled at the duke's dogged determination to continue on the subject. For a man with far greater concerns, he still wanted the club to run smoothly and its members to be content, even if it meant importing French champagne and lusty new wenches to serve it to mark the special occasion. "There is nothing wrong. I am merely weary tonight."

"Then take a room upstairs, claim some company if you've a mind for it, and get some rest. There is a wariness about your eyes that troubles me. Marinari can provide a sleeping draft if you require one."

Rafe nodded, thinking Marinari was the last woman he would ever request aid from. Mrs. Angela Marinari, the club's abbess for want of a better title, had a smooth tongue to tease and tempt a man. She was the only woman employed at the club with the power to arouse him with a single heated look. For a man who had discovered early in his life that women were not in the least tempting, the idea was profoundly unnerving. He'd given up longing to be like his friends some time ago. He hadn't even lied about bedding women in more than two years. "I'll consider it, I promise."

The duke appeared ready to say more until Lord Bracknell, the duke's heir and new proprietor of the club, hailed him. He excused himself and Rafe breathed a sigh of relief. Now there was a man ill-at-ease with decadence and excess. Rafe had only spoken to Lord Bracknell a few times since his involvement in the club had begun last year, and on each occasion the other man appeared deeply troubled by what went on around them.

Without the duke's company, Rafe found a chair in a quiet corner where he could be alone with the real source of his discontent. He couldn't very well confess to the duke that he was lonely even in a crowded room or intimate setting. No matter how great the pleasure his lovers at the club provided, a degree of guilt ate at him afterward. Perhaps that's why when he did partake, he rarely went back to the same man too soon.

He engaged in the pleasures afforded by his membership to the Hunt Club—a place where he was free to be himself and need not to fear the consequences of an incautious dalliance. His heart had never come close to strong involvement with any bed partner so far.

Havers, a footman and occasional willing bed partner, appeared at his elbow and deposited a drink that Rafe hadn't ordered yet. That was the way of things at the club. The servants came to know what a gentleman liked very well and were always on hand to provide immediate satisfaction. He murmured his thanks, ignoring the soft smile of invitation lighting his eyes, and sipped the brandy, thoughts turning to events earlier in the day and again experienced the stirrings of guilt.

Tonight's bed partner had thrilled him, reminded him

that his needs were best met when someone of his own sex writhed against him. Still, he wasn't entirely satisfied much beyond the moment of release. Like Havers, the young man he'd bedded had been very accommodating. He'd done everything Rafe had required and more.

He was beginning to fear that even when he'd found the perfect place to conduct his affairs with members of his own sex there wasn't much hope he ever would be entirely satisfied. He needed more.

He snatched up the paper and attempted to lose himself in the world of commerce and politics. Yet it was no use. He was quite bored by it all.

With the paper before him, hiding him almost completely from those engaged in conversation, Rafe studied his fellow patrons. Secret and not-so-secret alliances formed and dissolved with frequent adjustment in the club. This week, Lord Hitchins and Rubrick were not speaking to each other. Lord Harkness and the usually intense Lord Armitage had formed a surprising new friendship. Lord Lewes had actually smiled. A rare event. Perhaps his time abroad on the Continent had done him some good.

It constantly amazed him how some members barely acknowledged each other outside the club yet were so intimately involved in each other's lives within. How intimately he didn't need to speculate on because it was really none of his business.

It intrigued him, though, where he discovered liaisons existed between other lords. He'd concluded that such close ties were in no small part thanks to the Hunt Club's strict rules of exploring every pleasure a body could withstand in total expectation of secrecy. The club's code of honor demanded that each member, and even employee, sign the registrar upon entering the establishment for the first time. After that, the patrons were never likely to risk exposure because to risk others meant to risk them all.

A throat cleared at his side and Rafe lowered the paper he wasn't reading.

"Excuse the intrusion, Lord Raphael," Baily, the club's

majordomo, apologized as he held out a silver tray containing a solitary calling card. "A message has come for you."

Rafe picked it up and his pulse leapt. "When was this delivered?"

"Not two minutes ago, my lord. A young man delivered it and is waiting for a response. Do you wish to acknowledge you are here?"

"Of course." Rafe discarded the newssheet to the closest low table, tugged his waistcoat down and smoothed his hair. "Have Lord Claymore's carriage wait. My hat and gloves quickly, Bailey."

A sense of intense happiness gripped him and Rafe struggled to keep the smile from his face. Claymore was in London again. It had been far too long since he'd seen or heard from his best friend. He'd just started to consider taking a trip to Claymore's estate in Sussex to see if the man's mama had chained him there, or worse gotten him married off.

He hurried for the front door, collected his possessions, and strode down the front stairs eagerly, peering into the darkness for the earl's coach and livery. He didn't see it. A Hunt Club footman standing beside the doorway pointed down the street to a plain dark hack. He hurried toward it, puzzled not to see Claymore's coachman's familiar face at the reins. But then again he'd never bear driving a carriage that wasn't the finest quality. He nodded politely. "Good evening. Do you have Lord Claymore in there?"

"Indeed I do. Evening, sir."

A shabby groom opened the door and Rafe plunged into the darkened interior quickly. Unfortunately, he fell heavily against Claymore, hands and arms tangling. "Excuse me," he muttered, grasping a handful of earl and enjoying every stolen moment. "Where the devil is your brougham?"

"Elsewhere," Claymore replied as he dragged Rafe upright and caught him in a rare embrace. "Rafe. It's good to see you. If you're so put out about the carriage then what the devil are you grinning like a loon for?"

Rafe did his best to keep the embrace as brotherly as possible even as he soaked in every detail, scent, warmth, and a near overpowering longing. Reluctantly, he released Claymore and found a place on the opposite side of the carriage. After a moment, his eyes adjusted to the dim interior and he could see his friend was dressed to go out, probably to the Sanderson ball as most patrons of the club had done. "Your arrival saved me a trip to Sussex for your birthday. Couldn't let the milestone pass without celebrating it. But this is so much better with you in London. You know how well your mother and I get along."

Claymore snorted and leather creaked as he made himself more comfortable against the squabs. "You and the rest of the world." After a long pause, he cocked his head. "Was all that smile for my arrival?"

"Well not all," Rafe said quickly, scrambling for a believable excuse to explain his joy. It wouldn't do to admit to the depths of longing suffered these past months. He grinned at Claymore as he remembered a bet they'd made months ago. "Lord Carmichael's wife is pregnant so you owe me ten pound."

One of Claymore's dark eyebrows rose at the news. "Is she now? But who is the father?"

Rafe laughed and stretched his legs before him. When his knee knocked into Claymore's he pretended it was accidental and not a deliberate touch to tease himself with. "Barely matters and it wasn't part of the bet as to who filled her belly. Fair's fair. Settle the debt, Claymore."

"Actually, that's what I'm here to do."

When Claymore reached into his pocket and withdrew a handful of coins, Rafe gaped. He'd only been jesting. What the hell was this? "It wasn't in the least bit urgent."

"News does carry as far as Sussex." Claymore sighed deeply. "Debts must be settled."

Rafe collected the money and tucked it into his waistcoat pocket, mulling over the odd tone of Claymore's voice. "How long are you in London?"

"Just a few days then I'll be gone."

"But not before your birthday surely." Panic seized

him. A few days were not nearly long enough. "We must celebrate it together this year. It's not every day a man turns five and twenty."

"No, I intend to be here as long as my birthday."

He expelled the air he'd trapped in his lungs and his tension eased. "Good. I can make plans for the next week."

"I have a few things to do."

Damnation. If Claymore had brought his mother and younger sister, with him to London, Rafe would barely see him without their annoying company. He longed for just a little bit of time alone with him. Was that too much to ask of his lifelong friend? "Such as?"

Claymore sat up a little straighter, fussing with the fit of his tailcoat as if talking of his plans made him uncomfortable. He wasn't usually hesitant to talk about anything. "I wish to hire a punt and a man to take a trip on the Thames, and then sail downriver for some distance."

Rafe chuckled softly, remembering the last time they had attempted a voyage on the Thames. "Were we not going to do that two years ago, but it rained the whole week? If I remember correctly, we had planned to take Mrs. Hunter and Mrs. Craven for the journey." The plan to bed the lush widows under the stars with the waves gently rocking them had been an unexpectedly bold suggestion by Claymore. An event Rafe had wished for very much, if only to catch a glimpse of Claymore unbuttoned to enliven his private fantasies.

"Mrs. Hunter's company is not a requirement for me this year, however, I still wish to go if you'd care to accompany me." Claymore paused a long moment before he continued. "You can bring Mrs. Craven if you wish."

He studied Claymore closely. There was an odd catch to his friend's voice tonight. Rafe had never known him to be so glum on his arrival in London before. He was always serious, but perhaps there was more to his troubles at the estate than his infrequent letters had indicated. Rafe would do his best to get to the bottom of it and offer whatever paltry assistance within his means. He deliberately nudged Claymore's leg again. "It wouldn't be the same without Mrs. Hunter keeping you company.

We can go together without company. In fact, I'd prefer it."

"You wouldn't mind?"

Rafe nodded. "Of course not. It will be like when we were boys and rowing on the river near your estate."

Claymore snorted. "Except this time someone with more competence will do the navigation for us."

He laughed at the mention of their last, and near disastrous, boating expedition. "Exactly." He leaned forward to slap Claymore's thigh firmly. "What could possibly go wrong with a competent man at the helm?"

Claymore knocked his hand away as if his touch was offensive. "It's my hope you stay dry this time."

Rafe bit his lip, cursing his wandering hands. Wishing to touch Claymore would only lead to frustration and risk exposure. His friend was strictly a skirt chaser. He'd likely never considered anything more adventurous. Touching a man intimately would offend his sensibilities.

The carriage turned a sharp corner and Rafe peered out into the street. "Where are we going?"

"Lisbon's. I need a drink."

Not for the first time, Rafe regretted that Claymore wasn't a member of the Hunt Club. Lisbon's was clean enough and had a certain charm that had appealed when he'd first come up to Town, but it also had an unstable element on most nights that Rafe would rather avoid. It wasn't that he couldn't fight to defend himself, it was just that he preferred not to need to when he was engaged in serious drinking.

The calm serenity and companionable atmosphere of the Hunt Club appealed to him far better these days. Maybe he was getting older and wiser. Rafe set his boot heels to the seat opposite and made himself comfortable for the remaining journey. The only good thing about Claymore not being a member of the Hunt Club was that he had no opportunity to learn Rafe's preferred choice in bed partner. If he discovered that, Rafe doubted they'd remain on good terms. Claymore was frustratingly conservative in every respect. He withheld a sigh of disappointment. "A drink is just what we need."

CHAPTER TWO

James surveyed the crowded hell with a feeling of discontent and resignation. There was nothing different with his surroundings from any other night he'd been here, only he had changed too much to ever be the same man again. Discovering he didn't know himself as well as he should was a struggle to comprehend–one that had proved impossible to come to terms with over the past few months he'd hidden himself away at Claymore, pretending to be busy when he really wasn't.

But a gentleman must know himself and what he'd discovered gave him few palatable choices.

He leaned close to Rafe's ear. "There's an ugly mood tonight. Stay close."

At his side, his best friend, and closest confidant since they'd both been sent to the same school as boys, eased a touch closer, a hand settling on James's forearm. "Of course, but should you like to go somewhere else?"

James tossed back his drink and called for another. "No need. This place has everything I need." He swallowed the next glass set before him, determined to end the night in a drunken haze. He had always set goals and planned out his life to the last detail. Why not ensure that every last one was done before he died. Getting drunk one last time, preferably in Rafe's safe company, was a priority.

Maybe one of the hell's patrons' fists could beat some sense into him before he got to the second to last goal.

Another glass appeared before him, but Rafe snatched it away. "This isn't like you. What's going on?"

James glanced around them. He couldn't ever speak of what troubled him. It was usually Rafe who behaved irresponsibly and thought little of his reputation. What would his friend say if he knew how dark and muddied James' mind had become this past year? "Nothing. Can't a man enjoy a glass or two in peace?"

Rafe's frown grew. "He can, as long as he promises not to do it too often."

A smile tugged at his lips. Such a promise was easy to make. There was little time left. "No, this will be the last, I'm sure."

His friend slid the glass across the tabletop and James reached for it. Oblivion. One night to forget everything and then he would face the next few days with a clear head and unwavering determination. Yes, that was exactly what he needed to do.

A heavy weight slammed into James' back and he lurched forward into Rafe. Again, those odd cravings surfaced and he gave thanks that the alcohol could explain his imbalance. His reluctance to release Rafe would have raised eyebrows in any other establishment. Eventually, he pushed away and turned around to see who'd had the nerve to fall upon him.

Yet it wasn't just him the one fellow had fallen into. It seemed the hell had gone mad while James' back was turned. The press of bodies surged violently toward the far wall, leaving himself and Rafe untouched for the present. It wouldn't last longer than a moment.

His head cleared quickly and James grabbed Rafe's arm as the swell of bodies changed direction toward them. His friend may not be as strong or as well versed in fisticuffs as him, but he would not hold his own if they were overwhelmed like this. "Time to leave."

"I think that might be wise." Rafe offered a lopsided grin that never failed to make James feel like the most unworthy man who had ever lived. With the doorway blocked by fighters, James dodged a pair arguing over a busty lass and steered Rafe away from others. Once they were past the violence, he looked for another exit. A window would even suffice.

Rafe tugged on his arm. "What are you doing?"

"Getting us out of here without the pain."

Rafe glanced behind them. "I'd appreciate that."

Guilt ate at James for the disappointment and hurt he'd inflict on Rafe soon. By staying away, he'd hoped to resolve his problem. Unfortunately, there seemed little he could do to change himself back into the man he and his friend expected. "I should have invited you down to Claymore, though I had barely a moment to spare for entertainment."

His friend would never understand the change in him. When Rafe smiled ruefully, James' chest tightened in panic. He wished Rafe would not smile so much. The action made his last goal so much harder to consider.

"If you had invited me down I might have seen proof with my own eyes that you were actually engaged in work," Rafe teased.

James pushed him toward the rear of the building. "How's your father?"

"Unbearably difficult. Under the hatches constantly." Rafe grimaced. "I think he may be truly ill this time."

James wasn't entirely surprised by the news. Rafe's father, Lord Norwich, was a hard man and in illness his temper was even more difficult and argumentative. Rafe had written many a long letter in the past months, complaining of his father's high-handed ways, his stepmother's simpering and cosseting. Without James, Rafe had said life was dull. The exaggerated statement had made James regret what must be done even more.

He steered Rafe around a group with a slight nudge to his shoulder but then snatched his hand back. It had been many months since they'd seen each other and when he had laid eyes on Rafe tonight he'd experienced a stab of relief and intense attraction to the man. Yet Rafe was the same as he'd always been. Nothing had changed his friend's state of mind in the past months. Nothing yet, anyway.

Peace reigned at the rear of the establishment and James reconsidered the need to do so soon. He found a quiet corner where the press of their fellow man was less stifling and since it sounded as if the fight had subsided he signaled a footman to bring them new drinks. He leaned close to Rafe so he wouldn't be overheard. "Estate was a bloody mess. I swear, there were bats in my bedchamber on the first night. You wouldn't have lasted more than a night."

Rafe's lips lifted into a grin caused warmth to bloom in his chest. "I'd certainly have outlasted your estimation. But then I would have let you deal with the little monsters and sat back to watch you at work. It is your estate, after all."

James peered at Rafe through narrowed eyes. "I thought you were my friend."

"The best." He slung his arm about James's shoulders. "But I also know what battles to fight and when prudence and retreat would be the safest path. Let's face facts; you like to control everything in your life. Not that I have any objections to your managing ways, but truthfully, getting you to see another option as valid is akin to paddling upriver in a leaky punt. You do usually get everything you set your heart on. Not all of us are so fortunate to have such liberty."

James stared at his drink and gritted his teeth rather than answer. Yes, that would be how Rafe saw him. There was nothing wrong in his statement. Yet, for the right incentive he might be persuaded to change his mind.

Rafe dropped his arm slowly.

James saw a fleeting glimpse of uncertainty in Rafe's eyes. He smiled quickly and glanced away, revealing his lean profile—the bones of his face were even sharper since the last time they'd been together. Attraction filled James with deep unease. He shouldn't want to reach over and hold Rafe's face in his palm. He should not want to lick those full lips and thrust his tongue past them. Both were impossible dreams.

Despite his intentions for the week in London, he wanted nothing to mar his time with Rafe. Companionable moments were all he could expect. Rafe may flit from idea to idea, one skirt to another, so quickly that James couldn't keep his lovers' names straight, but his friend was a constant he relied upon. "Please don't remind me how fortunate I am again. Once the house is rendered livable, my mother will demand I host a house party. She tells me it's high time I married."

When their drinks were refreshed, Rafe drank his straight down. "That again," he said bitterly.

"'Tis a subject Mama is intent on pursuing." James sipped his, intrigued by his friend's sudden irritation with the frequent topic of conversation between them. Neither of them was keen to become leg-shackled. James had finally figured out why the notion didn't appeal to him and why he'd put the decision aside for so long.

He simply didn't crave a woman's touch as other men did.

Rafe called the footman over and had his glass replenished. "When do you think Claymore will be ready for visitors?"

"I've put Mama off for a few months yet." His heart clenched. The timing would depend on how long his family mourned and whether the next Lord Claymore permitted Mama and his sister to remain. "When there is a house party to attend, my sister will expect you to come. I'm sure you'll find it tedious, but Caitlin will appreciate your company and support. You know how much she hates meeting new people."

Rafe frowned. "That will make it a painful enterprise to launch her on Society this year."

"Next year," James corrected. A sudden apprehension filled him. He wouldn't be here to help her find her feet in Society. Although Rafe didn't realize it yet, James was counting on him to ease Caitlin's way in his stead. The pair had always gotten along. She would listen to Rafe's advice. "Caitlin will do fine, I am sure. She'll just need to see a friendly face and a bit of time to get her bearings." He grinned. "You'll dance with her, I trust."

His friend rolled his eyes. "Of course I will, but she won't thank me for abusing her toes afterward."

"Thank you." He swallowed quickly as raw emotion choked him.

Rafe's grin returned. "Somewhere out there a young lady should be grateful not to have the Earl of Claymore crush their toes too."

James punched Rafe's arm and returned the grin, putting aside his regrets for a few more days. "No matter how many dance lessons he took, Lord Raphael is just as clumsy with a girl in his arms as I am. Come on. Let's see what else is afoot."

He pushed Rafe ahead of him and they moved into a smoke-filled chamber where games of chance were being played. Inside, the level of conversation grew in volume, as did the crowd. To ensure he didn't become separated from Rafe, James kept as close as decently possible without actually hanging onto his friend.

Three steps further in, Rafe stopped suddenly, pivoted and crashed into James' chest. His eyes had widened in panic. "My brother is here."

"Ian?" James awkwardly righted Rafe and then jerked his hands back. He peeked over His friend's shoulders and saw a familiar shock of ginger hair across the room. Thankfully, Ian was watching the games not the crowd and hadn't seen them yet. "Damn. Last person I want to see tonight too. Why the devil is he in my favorite hell?"

"Don't know, but he's irritating me even more of late." Rafe pushed at his chest. "I think Father has bribed him to follow me about Town to make sure I'm keeping out of trouble."

James frowned at that, though he yielded to Rafe's insistent nudges to head in the opposite direction. "Why the hell would he do that after all these years?"

Rafe shrugged, but his gaze darted away as if there was a reason and didn't want to confess it. Although he'd like nothing better than to pry into Rafe's life, he'd wait until they'd lost the brother completely before he tried. "This way. I'm not having him shadow us all night."

James caught Rafe's hand and tugged. Their fingers tangled for a moment but swiftly parted. The warmth that crept over James took him by surprise. He clenched his fist to retain the sensation while Rafe rushed toward the rear of the building and hopefully another exit.

He followed close behind so he would not lose sight of his friend, glancing over his shoulder occasionally to see if they had been spotted and even now pursued. For the present, he could see no sign of Ian.

Unwilling to take any chances, he pushed Rafe down

the servants' stairs at the end of the corridor and into an unfamiliar part of the building. Maybe if they waited in the kitchens long enough, the brother would leave and they could venture upstairs again. Not spotting a kitchen, or even an exit, he and Rafe slipped inside a dark room and pressed their ears to the door, listening for sounds beyond.

Yet it wasn't long before James recognized other sounds, ones coming from behind them. Rough masculine groans and a repetitive squeak. He turned slowly, eyes widening at the situation they'd accidentally stumbled upon. Across the room, a man was tupping someone, the unseen body bent over a chair. As he squinted, he noticed two pair of trousers pooled at their feet. His gaze dipped to the man's arse, watching the full white flesh flex. His pulse soared, confirming his worst fears were all too true.

He stared at the bare arse and strong muscled thighs pumping in and out of the man trapped beneath and desperately wanted to be one of them. He didn't care which. He drew in a shaky breath. One day, he would experience that forbidden pleasure for himself. Just once on his last day on earth.

He risked a quick glance at Rafe to see his reaction to such a scene. Rafe's gaze was fixed on the couple, too, his lips parted in surprise. Was he shocked? Would he cry out in alarm and draw attention to the pair. Rafe's tongue darted out to wet his lips and a soft sound left him.

James lowered his gaze to determine exactly how disturbing Rafe found the scene. To his surprise his friend's breeches had tented with an impressive bulge. One James discovered he wanted to cup and bring to his mouth.

He gulped back the horror of that thought and glanced at the lovers. Unfortunately, they had realized they had company and had frozen in place. The uppermost gentleman came to his senses and quickly jerked up his breeches, face mottled with rage or from his exertions, fists clenched.

"Excuse us," Rafe said quickly as he caught James' arm. He pushed him toward a window left ajar on the far side of the room. "Just looking for the quickest way out. Don't mind us." Without another word, Rafe shoved James through the window. They fell into a lane, one that reeked of refuse and human waste and quickly brushed themselves off.

They were alone. James risked another peek at Rafe. He was still aroused. Despite that, Rafe grinned and at the first hint of voices behind them, he urged James into a run.

CHAPTER THREE

Rafe pounded up the darkened lane, sliding on the slick cobblestones in his haste to avoid any pursuers and his embarrassment, his head throbbing with the beginnings of yet another headache. Behind him, Claymore's rough pant both reassured him that he was not alone but his presence also heightened his panic. He hoped Claymore hadn't noticed he'd become aroused by the scene they'd stumbled on.

He didn't normally find thrill in watching others make love, but that sleekly muscled arse had tempted him. Probably because the Earl of Claymore had stood beside him, lapping up the decadence of the scene without a word of protest or shock.

Ahead, a hackney carriage rumbled past the end of the lane, appearing empty of passengers.

"Catch that," Claymore urged.

Rafe pushed himself harder, legs burning with the effort. "Wait," he called to the driver. The muffled shape at the reins turned at his voice but didn't slow.

Claymore drew ahead, his longer legs easily eating up the distance. He caught the side of the hackney and threw the door open. "We've the fare, never fear," he told the spluttering driver, as he dug into his pocket for coin.

The old man grunted and marginally slowed.

He dived in, only to reappear a moment later, hand outstretched for Rafe to take. With a renewed burst of speed, Rafe caught it and Claymore hauled him inside the slowly moving darkened conveyance. He landed on top of Claymore, stunned, aroused, his face hot with embarrassment. Claymore jerked beneath him. Rafe scrambled to the other side of the carriage and attempted to catch his breath.

"Green Street," Rafe called out before latching the door closed and collapsing back against the squabs. "Well, that was an interesting evening."

Claymore glanced out the window, his mouth twisting as if he was fighting anger. "I'll say. The door did have a latch."

Rafe leaned his head against the squabs, attempting to appear unperturbed. He willed his erection to subside. "True."

"I have an odd question to ask." Claymore cleared his throat. "Did you feel the urge to report them to the authorities? They'd hang for that."

His face grew hot. He squinted across at his conservative friend in dread. Sodomites were prosecuted and publicly hanged if found guilty. Two lords swearing they'd caught two strangers in the act would be believed readily. Rafe would not take part in such a trial. He was as guilty as anyone who preferred to be buggered. "Is it any of my business?" He squinted at Claymore. "Do you mind if we continue this discussion another time?"

"Of course." His friend rubbed his hand across his jaw and then sighed heavily. "Why are we going to my home?"

Rafe rubbed his temple as the pounding headache grew in strength. "Quietest place I know to talk to you. I could invite you home for a drink, but I'm unwilling to spar with my father tonight. Bellows like a bull in the stocks. He's not been well and I've got a damned headache now." He was feeling uncommonly concerned about his father's health for the first time in his life. The man was built like an ox and to be anything but rudely sound was a sign of frailty he couldn't reconcile. Perhaps it was simply because he felt so bloody miserable himself. His headache grew worse than ever as the rough hack threw him about.

Claymore squeezed his thigh. "Nothing serious, I hope."

Rafe shrugged. "He's refused to see a physician. I'm sure he'll recover his strength in a few days."

"I was talking about you." Claymore rubbed Rafe's thigh in soothing circles. "Would you prefer to go home and rest? We can catch up another night."

"God, no. There's no rest to be had at home.

Stepmother gives me little peace these days."

"Very well. We'll be there soon."

He closed his eyes, savoring the sensations caused by Claymore's hand on his leg, and fighting off the feeling he might cast up his accounts at any moment due to the sway of the hack. The exertion of the run on top of his aching head made him feel so dreadful he honestly didn't care where he was going. Claymore was with him and while he should shake off the touch, he felt so damn miserable that he couldn't bring himself to move his leg away.

Rafe swallowed and searched his mind for a familiar and safe subject. "Its days like these that I envy your freedom to do as you please. Do you know how hard it is to find a private moment?"

Claymore finally slid his hand away. "I can."

After years of such friendly touches, Rafe should not have hoped for more. But he had never managed to turn aside his dangerous thoughts for his friend. He had to be careful to hide his desires. Their friendship, and his very life, depended on keeping his attraction to men secret. Especially around Claymore.

When his friend fell silent for the rest of the journey, Rafe tried his best to be content. However, he couldn't help sneaking peaks at Claymore's profile. The earl was attractive in his own serious way and also the most unreadable. His broad shoulders, achieved from weekly bouts of boxing against a servant, dwarfed Rafe's slender body. Not that he minded. He'd long given up hoping to match Claymore's bulk years ago.

Claymore's eyes, though turned away now, were a startling shade of blue that sparkled when he spoke. Rafe caught himself on the cusp of a smitten sigh. Behavior of that kind was not wise. But what he wouldn't give to have those brilliant blue orbs staring at him with unguarded passion instead of concern.

He jumped as Claymore shook him. "Coming in or should I send the carriage toward home?"

Rafe blinked in confusion. "What happened?"

"You dozed off." The earl frowned and stepped out onto

the street. He paid the fare and caught Rafe when he stumbled out. Rafe's legs trembled with the effort to stand. "When did you eat last?"

"Breakfast," he assured him. But he hadn't eaten a great deal. "I've not had much of an appetite of late. Stepmother's new chef leaves much to be desired."

Claymore led him into the darkened town house and closed the door behind them. He lit a candle but did not call out to the night footman or butler for assistance. "Go on into the sitting room and I'll see what's to be had. You must eat. You're as white as a sheet."

Rafe stumbled into the room and collapsed onto a chaise. Hell, he was suddenly so tired he could curl up here and now. He couldn't fall asleep yet. Claymore had only just returned to London. He sat up quickly and his head cracked into Claymore's, reigniting the pounding in his skull. His friend cursed and held his head too. "Hell's bells, that hurts."

"Sorry," he mumbled. "Perhaps it might be better if I just stay still." He slumped back into the well-padded chaise with the delicacy of an ox and caught his bottom lip between his teeth as the room slowly revolved around him.

Claymore briefly cupped his cheek and then brushed his hand over his forehead. "I think so too or else there will be no one whole to take care of either of us. What's wrong with you?"

Rafe could only shrug for an answer. He was too distracted by Claymore's touch.

When he slipped away, Rafe groaned and glanced around the familiar chamber. The rest of the furniture was still covered by white cloths. He listened carefully, detecting no other sounds save his own breathing. The house was eerily silent and he'd be concerned if Claymore wasn't near. Empty houses were an oddity that usually scared him, though he'd never admit to that out loud. He scooted into a more comfortable position and closed his eyes for a moment.

When Claymore returned, Rafe was almost too sleepy to acknowledge it, but he managed to pull himself upright and squinted across at his friend. "Where are your servants?"

"Ah, never mind that now." He slid the tray onto Rafe's lap and stood back. "The best I could manage on short notice."

The food on the tray was an odd mixture of biscuit, fruit and turnip. "Maybe later," he mumbled, keeping a firm grip on his stomach as he considered the odd combination. Cook must be foxed to have sent up this. The buzzing in his head increased and he pressed the heel of his hand against his temple.

The filled tray rattled as it slid from his legs to a side table and then Claymore sat pressing his hand to Rafe's skin repeatedly as a wave of heat swept him. "You really are unwell."

Regardless of the danger, he leaned into Claymore's hand and slumped into his embrace. "So it would seem. Sorry to put a damper on your evening, my friend, but I fear I'm not much use tonight."

A glass was pressed to his lips and he swallowed and then scowled. Claymore had given him water. Even that small consumption had his stomach rolling. He pushed at the earl's hand to move the glass away. "No more."

Claymore's humph reached him.

Rafe patted his leg. "I'll come good tomorrow. You'll see. I just need a bit of sleep."

"I suppose." Claymore's hand settled over his. "I'd feel better if you'd stay."

The idea of not moving, or not moving far, held a great appeal at the moment especially if he had more opportunities to touch his best friend. Maybe he should have *fallen ill* more often in the past. Who knows how far he could have progressed with Claymore then. Thinking it best not to appear too eager, he shrugged. "I should go home and allow my stepmother to do the job she always claimed to love but never carried out."

"That woman only cares for Ian, and we both know how much attention you'll receive from her. You'd be better off here or with strangers."

Rafe pressed a hand to his stomach as it rolled

uncomfortably. "Perhaps I should stay. Will you send a note round to my father in the morning? He'll only worry more than he needs to. I don't know why he insists I start each day sharing a meal together."

"Of course I can send a note. I'd do it now but…"

He allowed Claymore to ease him to his feet. When the earl slid his arm about Rafe's waist he tried not to moan at how good it felt to be held. By the midpoint of the staircase, Claymore almost carried him. A heavy sweat broke out over his skin everywhere, making the journey seem unreasonably difficult. Yet Claymore's strong arms anchored him, even when the world began to slowly spin in the most disconcerting way.

At the top of the stairs, he was surprised when Claymore led him into his own bedchamber. His friend eased Rafe onto the wide bed and he sighed. He'd been waiting for a moment like this, climbing into Claymore's bed, all his life, and he was too ill to appreciate the honor. The bed was soft, linen cool and the man before him gentle.

Rafe sank down unresisting, aware that his best friend undressed him. He was content to be ordered about as if he was a child because it was Claymore and he trusted him with his life. He struggled to keep his eyes open as Claymore arranged his limbs beneath the covers.

CHAPTER FOUR

James slipped into his bedroom and breathed a sigh of relief to see Rafe twitching in the bed. "I thought I heard you."

Rafe turned over in the rumpled bed and faced him, exposing the sleek upper portion of his body that he had touched fleetingly last night. "I cannot account for my weariness. It is completely unfair that your bed, which you've rarely used of late, appears far more comfortable than mine ever has."

Relieved that Rafe was capable of complaining over inconsequential matters, James crossed the room and sank into the chair he'd placed beside the bed. He didn't mind that Rafe was still here, still reclining in his bedroom with every appearance of not wishing to leave it. His friend had given him an anxious, sleepless night. He knew nothing of illness or treatments and had been on the point of leaving in search of a physician when he'd heard Rafe moving about the room. "You look rather better than last night. How do you feel?"

The line that had creased his forehead and the squint with which he had surveyed his surroundings had disappeared after a full and deep sleep.

"Rather foolish." A rueful smile twisted Rafe's lips. "Perhaps I just needed a decent night's rest."

"Possibly." James willed himself to relax. His friend would be fine. There was no need to worry himself. Rafe always landed on his feet. "Are you hungry?"

"Famished. Tell Cook to send up two of everything."

He stood and moved to the window to peer out. He didn't currently have a cook to spoil him or his friend with, but as he'd come up the stairs he'd thought he'd heard a pie seller call out from the street. What luck. One lingered outside his town house still. "Excuse me."

Without waiting for a reply, he hurried outside and

paid for four beef pies. Two for each of them. It was the best he could manage without wandering too far afield.

When he returned to his bedchamber, Rafe was standing beside the bed. "Where are your servants?"

James dragged his gaze up to his friend's face rather than salivate over the bare chest and smalls that hinted at the anatomy beneath. "I dismissed them all yesterday."

Rafe sank onto the bed edge. "Thievery?"

"No. I don't want to talk about it if you don't mind. This is the best I can do on short notice."

"Why not?" Rafe took a pie from him and enthusiastically bit into it. "I've never gossiped about your affairs before."

James placed the remaining pies on a table and bit into his own. He'd dismissed the servants because very soon they would not have an employer to tend and he wished to spare his mother and sister the expense. There was much to be said for tying up loose ends at the end of one's life. At least he'd accomplished something last night that he hadn't planned. He'd spent part of the night in the same bed as a man he found attractive. It didn't matter that nothing intimate had happened between them and that he'd dozed above the sheets, while listening to Rafe's surprisingly loud snore. When he'd woken, he'd felt rather more pleased with himself than he had for a very long time.

He jumped as Rafe grasped his shoulder. "James," he murmured behind him, close enough that his breath skimmed his ear. "Tell me what's on your mind. It's not like you to keep secrets from me."

When Rafe continued to hold him in place, James sighed. As much as he wished otherwise, he'd known he couldn't avoid the subject entirely, not with Rafe. "I'm tired of everything being the same as it ever was. I want things to be different. To be what I want rather than what I must be."

His friend moved closer. He brushed his hand up and down James' arm until he couldn't breathe. "What more do you want for your life, Jimmy?"

He spluttered and turned about. "No one has called

me that in years."

One of Rafe's eyebrows arched high. "It suits you better than Claymore ever has and I much prefer it. We are friends. Can you tolerate it when we are alone?"

James held himself still. He couldn't remember when exactly Rafe had ceased calling him Jimmy, but he had to admit he had missed the informality. Rafe was the one man, one friend, he could count on not to laugh at him. They'd been through so much together. If he went through with his plan, that would change. He nodded.

Rafe grinned suddenly. "You know, I never liked that Simmons fellow you had at your door so I won't miss him. Such a starched shirt for a butler, too high in the instep, always throwing his disapproval in our faces when we returned from a particularly good night on the town." He frowned. "I will miss your cook, though."

"Are you still hungry?"

"Ravenous," he said with a grin. "In fact, once we eat all of those I think you and I should count our blessings. One, we are together again and two, there is no one about to spy on what we do. Do you realize this is the first time in years I have been entirely alone?"

James poked his chest, affronted by being overlooked. "You're not quite alone."

"Jimmy, I am alone with you, my oldest and most trusted friend. How could life be better? If you'll lend me a change of garments we can go out to snare ourselves a proper meal. I have the appetite of a horse that must be satisfied with something substantial." Rafe threw his arm about James' shoulders. "Then once we are replete, we can go to the theatre, the opera, damn it all even Covent Garden to snare us a pair of fetching wenches to warm your bed tonight."

James sighed. One last night with his best friend, but he didn't want anything to do with women. Could he trust himself hide the truth a little longer?

When he didn't immediately agree, Rafe drew close, a frown marring his brow. "You said you wanted things to be different," Rafe said, then chewed his lower lip as if he were indeed anxious. "You were not bored with my company, were you, Jimmy?"

He struggled to lift his gaze from Rafe's full lower lip that had grown redder. The problem with lusting after your best friend is that they were used to being told the truth instantly. Any hesitation or half-truths were noticed. "Never. If not for you, I don't know what kind of man I'd be."

Rafe lifted a hand to James' head and drew him into an embrace. His grip was tight and he held their heads together for a long time. James hesitated a moment before he stroked down Rafe's spine. Rafe's bare back was warm and skin so soft. This might be the last time he'd ever have the opportunity so he savored every moment.

"Sentimental and foolish my father would say if he could see us together," Rafe confessed as he drew back. He grinned suddenly and then leaned forward to lay a fast, hearty kiss full on James's mouth. "I'd be lost without you too."

Rafe pivoted and stalked to James' dressing room without another word while James stood still in shock. He lifted a hand to his lips and brushed his fingers over them. They tingled with warmth and when he licked them, he searched for Rafe's taste. He lowered his hand and let out a shuddering breath. There, one more goal crossed off his list. He only had to enjoy a boating trip on the Thames with Rafe and he could die with what little dignity he had left.

CHAPTER FIVE

Rafe stripped his clothing from his body and rifled through James' possessions. Today wasn't the first time he'd borrowed his friend's clothes, but it was the first time he'd done so after kissing the man. He cursed his foolishness and willed his cockstand to subside before James had the opportunity to notice. He didn't want to ruin the strange mood that had sprung between them.

He found a shirt and drew it over his head. Thankfully, it fell well below his groin and hid his lingering erection. He turned to see what James was up to and found him standing in the doorway, his gaze fixed on Rafe's legs. Rafe swallowed, praying that the impulsive kiss hadn't been a mistake and that he'd not revealed his true desires. "Trousers?"

"To your left."

Of course they are. James was nothing if not predictable. He spread his fingers over James' clothing and chose a pair he hoped would fit. The man had excellent taste, but his body was a touch wider than his. Thinking of the difference between their figures threatened to sabotage his control of his lust, so he pulled a pair on quickly, casting an anxious eye over his shoulder. "Are you going to watch or valet for me?"

"Neither. Excuse me a moment." James turned away. "There is something I must do."

When James could no longer be heard, Rafe set a hand to the wall to steady himself. He had to do better than this. He knew how to hide his desires, of course. He had buried his yearnings for years, yet today James wasn't making it very easy to accomplish. He'd have to keep up his guard for the duration of his friend's stay in London.

He dressed quickly in the borrowed garments but slid on his own footwear. James had unbelievably long feet—

a subject that fascinated him and had given him ample material for teasing over the years. The earl had secured his place in the world in no small part to the space he occupied. His presence always lit up a room and many an eye followed his movements.

When he saw James hadn't returned to the bedchamber yet, Rafe wandered to the head of the stairs. He glanced down the stairwell, and spied James sitting on a bench seat beneath him, his head held in his hands. Rafe sprinted down the stairs, stopping only as he reached Jimmy. He pulled his friend up to face him. His eyes were wide. Panicked.

"Here now. What's the matter?" Rafe grasped his forearms arms tightly. "Jimmy, what the hell is going on with you? Tell me. Are your pockets to let?"

"It's nothing."

He shook him. "I don't believe that for a moment."

When the earl remained mute, Rafe crowded him against a wall. Up close, he heard his rushed breathing. He touched his face to see if he was fevered, but Jimmy closed his eyes and leaned his head against the wall. "There's nothing you can do."

"The hell there isn't. I'm your friend."

Jimmy rocked his head from side to side. "You wouldn't be my friend if you knew."

Rafe curled his fingers into his coat and held him, afraid of what Jimmy withheld. "Make sense, man."

"The kiss." The other man's throat worked as he swallowed. "The kiss makes everything final."

Rafe's heartbeat quickened. He'd given himself away. Surely there was a way to fix this. Dredging up a bravado he didn't feel, he firmly shook his head. "That was nothing. I apologize if I offended you."

"I wasn't offended," Jimmy whispered. "I liked it,"

Rafe drew back in shock, staring at his friend and unable to believe what he'd heard. He couldn't have said he liked the kiss. "What did you say?"

The earl opened his eyes and they were as wild as Rafe had ever seen them. "You heard me the first time.. Don't make me repeat it or I'll have no honor left."

He stepped forward, pressed a hand to Jimmy's chest, felt the erratic beat of the heart beneath his fingertips while trying desperately to understand. Jimmy had *liked* being kissed by a man? By *him*? How was that possible? The fellow was a confirmed skirt chaser. He had always had a mistress, long before Rafe had invented his lovers to disguise his frequent disappearances in search of prohibited pleasure.

But if Jimmy had liked the kiss and was near to tears over it then he couldn't possibly have a clue about Rafe's preferences. He was torturing himself for no reason. He may think they shouldn't indulge their urges, but this development made their attachment all too important.

He stepped closer, determined to get to the truth. Jimmy plastered himself against the wall. The other man glanced left and right. They were alone. There were no servants to catch them touching. No one would ever know what they did today. He raised his hand to Jimmy's face and scraped his nails over the hard stubble. "We will always be friends and do you know why?"

His friend shook his head.

"Because we like the same things. Boating, claret not port, a long vigorous ride." He pressed his forehead to Jimmy's, heart pounding with anxiety. "I didn't mind kissing you. In fact, I'd like to do so again and not be so quick about it this time. May I?"

When Jimmy's gaze fixed on Rafe's mouth, his pulse leaped. There was no disgust or alarm at his suggestion. He leaned close and brushed his lips against Jimmy's. A low growl sounded from his throat.

"Relax. I won't hurt you," Rafe whispered before he kissed the other man more firmly, forcing his tongue into his friend's mouth.

Jimmy clutched at his hips, dragging him closer against his larger body. Encouraged that he wasn't about to be pushed away, Rafe looped his arms over Jimmy's broad shoulders and rubbed his body against him. Instantly, he was spun about until his back was pressed firmly against the hall wall. The kisses grew wild, teeth, tongues, and lips hungering, striving to win a battle of wills. Rafe did not mind an aggressive man and found much pleasure in a firm handling. Especially not when it was his best friend, finally revealing a part of himself he had never expected to exist.

Eventually, Jimmy drew back, questions clear in his eyes, chest heaving.

Rafe didn't doubt he would fail to answer most to his immediate satisfaction, so he answered the one that mattered to him. "I've wondered about that kiss my whole life." He curled his arm tighter about his neck and pressed a kiss to his brow while he waited to see how Jimmy took the news.

The earl swallowed. He glanced down as his chest heaved. "Can there be more?"

CHAPTER SIX

As soon as the question passed his lips, James' fears spiked. He shouldn't have asked for more. Hell, he shouldn't have kissed his friend at all. He was so conflicted. Confused and near to panic. What if he ruined their friendship?

Rafe's face grew serious, a rare expression that under normal circumstances. "What more can there be, Jimmy?"

Rafe's question caused a sweat to form over his skin. The image of the couple they'd stumbled on in rut flickered through his mind. Yes, he wanted that. To bugger Rafe. To be inside his closest friend and hear him moan his name. Yet that wasn't an easy matter to confess. Rafe wasn't like him. He'd always chased women. He shook his head to deny his deepest desire even as Rafe curled his arm tighter about his neck and kissed him again, stroking his tongue firmly against his.

The persistence of the kiss took his breath away. Rafe had a talented tongue and used it to deepen the kiss into the most erotic one of his life. James pressed against him and touched him. The body against his was hard and long, exciting him with possibilities. He knew this body well, as well as his own, but never this way.

Rafe tangled his fingers in James' hair as he ground their hips together. His senses jumped as he realized he wasn't the only one excited. His friend had an erection prodding him too.

He slid his hands down Rafe's body and then up to delve beneath the loose-fitting coat. Rafe radiated warmth and James slid his hand low, slipping down to cup his arse. He held his breath. Rafe would stop him if he didn't want this.

Rafe moaned against his mouth and their kisses went from deep to untamed in an instant. The other man touched his chest, fumbling with his garments and teasing in a way he'd never experienced or expected to feel so deeply. Another kiss later, he detected a persistent tug at the buttons of his trousers, as Rafe burrowed inside them.

He gasped as Rafe gripped his length. There was no mistaking the difference from a woman's touch, and he liked the firmer handling better. Rafe's fingers encircled him at the base and then dragged upward. James groaned and pumped desperately into that touch.

For a few minutes, Rafe let him have his way, but then he took him in hand and teased and tugged and goaded his desires to extremes. A wild ache started in his cock, his breath came in huge struggling gasps.

He broke the kiss and knocked his hand away before the point of no return was reached. Rafe surprised him then by opening his own trousers, pushing them down his legs and taking himself in hand while James watched, mouth watering at the sight.

James stared at the puddle of fabric about their ankles, overcome with desire to fuck his friend. He placed his hand on Rafe's bare hip, squeezed then before he considered the matter again, he urged Rafe to turn around. The other man spun without protest, shrugging out of his coat as he went. The tails of his shirt covered his arse and James lifted them, shoving them beneath the waistcoat and out of the way.

Rafe's bare arse was beautiful—firm, white and so soft to touch. He caressed the skin, gently rubbing his knuckles over each perfect orb.

"Use this." Rafe shoved something at him, a flask of whiskey he assumed.

Brought to his senses, James handed it back. "I don't need a drink."

Rafe chuckled. "It's not for that. Put it on your cock. I assume you'd like to bugger me."

The blunt remark made him pant. He opened the flask and instead of spirit he found a slippery substance. Oil. The request took a moment to make perfect sense. Rafe was better prepared to be buggered than James had even considered he'd need to be. He poured some onto his hand, too much so that it flowed over his palm and spattered to the floor. He quickly coated his cock with the remainder, finding the sensation incredibly erotic. Something he'd never done before. He moved closer to Rafe and then stopped. It was one thing to want to bugger a man but entirely another to carry out the deed.

Rafe spread his feet as wide apart as was possible and wiggled his backside. He folded one arm upon the wall and rested his head upon it. "There's little difference."

How could he know exactly what James had been thinking? He drew closer and teased his oiled shaft against Rafe's perfect, round arse. His friend wriggled, chasing the sensations or so it appeared to James. He teased the tip of his cock into the crack and pressed forward.

Rafe sighed and reached back to draw his cheeks wider apart, presenting a view of his target. James pressed against that spot, still somewhat surprised by the unexpected opportunity. Rafe had always been willing to accommodate his wishes. But this he hadn't ever expected.

After momentary resistance, the head slipped inside. The tight grip, a thing he was unused to, made his hips jerk. He pushed in hard, body taking over his thinking as Rafe moaned. In and out, little by little, until he was half done, bound tight inside his best friend.

The tight squeeze was more than he imagined. It felt right to fuck Rafe. He caught Rafe's hip with his hand and heard another moan of want from his friend. James backed up and then thrust again.

By trial and error, he made love to Rafe, using the sounds his friend made as a guide to whether Rafe liked it. He curled a hand over Rafe's upper thigh and lifted his foot a little off the ground. The change cleared his way to press deeper, to move fully and to pound while he grunted to every thrust. With his other hand, he caught hold of his friend's cock and stroked him.

Rafe shouted out instantly, his hips and whole body jerking and tightening with the force of his release. The squeeze to his cock took his breath away and James spilled his seed, pumping madly and desperately inside Rafe. His world shook and smashed the remnants of his former self.

He'd suspected but not truly believed until now.

There was no turning aside from what he was.

A deep wave of sadness and futility rolled over him. He clung to Rafe, holding him tightly in his arms a little longer to retain those earlier feelings. He'd buggered a friend, used him to achieve his last wish. To find out for certain that his desires were real and not the product of a lonely mind.

Rafe raised one of James' hands to his mouth and kissed the back of it. "Thank you."

James drew back, disengaging from Rafe's arse so swiftly his cock stretched and snapped back against his thigh. He shouldn't be thanked for ruining Rafe's life. Rafe would hang along side him if they were ever found out.

CHAPTER SEVEN

The sudden loss of body heat sent a chill racing through Rafe. He shuffled around in time to catch a look of shame cross James' handsome face. The same one Rafe frequently saw in his own mirror, when he'd found pleasure in someone's arms and regretted his choice in bed partner. But this was different.

In place of shame and misery, hope bloomed in his chest and brought a smile. Today wasn't like any previous encounter. Today he'd been with the one he'd always wanted and he would make James see that there was nothing at all to regret. He tugged up his trousers enough that he could move toward James without stumbling. The earl retreated, backing away from him as if he expected punishment.

Rafe followed until his friend was halted by the staircase railing. "Are you all right?"

His face grew ashen. "How can you ask that? What I did was wrong."

"What you did was unbelievably right." Rafe speared his fingers into James' hair and gripped his head to prevent him from avoiding his gaze. "I loved it."

James' throat worked as he swallowed. "You did?"

He bent to the other man's throat and nibbled at his jaw. When he drew back with a final, quick kiss, he smiled. "Everything I ever wanted. I promise you that."

James looked at him skeptically. "You wanted to be taken against a wall by a beast?"

It seemed odd to Rafe that James wasn't experiencing the correct amount of bliss for so delightful a development. He placed both hands on the wall on either side of the other man's head and leaned close. "Having you bring me to release while you pound my arse is all I ever wanted. You are exciting to be around."

A sheepish smile tugged the corners of James' lips

and before another frown could replace it, Rafe kissed him. Kept kissing him for a further ten minutes since they couldn't be interrupted. When he drew back, James' frown had disappeared to be replaced by a look of distinct hunger.

Satisfied he'd made his point, he paused. "Let's go out for some air. I'm hungry and plan to be hungrier still later tonight."

James nodded. "Of course. I did forget we were going out."

"Now we can go out with a memory to tease us all the more." He skimmed his fingers over James' ear, and laughed when the man twisted out of his reach. James bent to draw up his trousers, a hesitant smile on his face. When he turned away, Rafe called after him. "Better find a mirror before we go out, Jimmy. I managed to destroy your cravat with my groping."

James pivoted, and then a slow smile formed. "You might be in need of one yourself. I do believe you'll need to borrow another set of my clothes."

As James hurried upstairs, Rafe glanced down. His cravat was lying on the floor, ripped in half. He hadn't the faintest idea when that had happened and he didn't mind. The cravat was James' after all. He remembered such similar emotions had struck him the first time he'd been with a man. The desperation would pass, and they had all the time in the world to share the rest together.

He shed his clothes as he entered James' room, pausing a moment to watch him at the washbasin. He breathed deep. He could die a happy man if this were his last breath and last view. James had shed his clothes too, and the play of muscles across his back sent a thrill through him. The man wanted him.

His trousers dropped low on his hips, and then to his thighs. Rafe caught his breath. He admired a firm arse and those two tight high cheeks clenched and flexed as he fussed at cleaning himself. Rafe gulped as his cock thickened.

He approached until he stood directly behind James. He stretched out his hands and swept them across the planes of the earl's back in a soft caress. "Can I assume that you didn't want women on our boating excursion because of what just happened between us?"

James clenched the tabletop before him, fingers tightening on the wood. "Yes."

He slid one hand up to James' nape, spanned the corded flesh, and squeezed firmly. "I didn't get to touch you very much before. Do you dislike it?"

"No." James sighed. "Quite the opposite."

Rafe held him in place when he would have turned. He knew this body well from his frequent observations, but he'd never done much more than embrace James through clothes. With no interruptions looming, Rafe was of a mind to forget his hunger and keep James all to himself. He stroked the earl's skin everywhere, rubbed his body against him when he could and discovered that his need to touch James was not easily appeased.

He dropped to his knees and took James' cock in hand. It was damp from being scrubbed in the wash water, and thick at the base tapering to a delicate tip. The ruddy length was full and hard because of Rafe's attention. Rafe opened his mouth and licked the head.

Above him, James gasped and clutched at his hair. "You shouldn't."

"And I won't. Not completely." He wasn't going to bring him to release again. But he had always liked to tease James. Now he simply had another means at his disposal. Rafe paid James' spluttering no mind, skimming his tongue over the smooth skin, teasing and hearing his lover's moans grow in strength. He licked his lips and then plunged James' cock into his mouth, reveling in his friend's startled yelp and the overwhelming urge to make love.

He slathered James' cock with his saliva and then moved his head along the length, taking him down to the back of his throat and out again. The long sucks and full retreat allowed him a taste of James's salty seed. A taste he'd dreamt of for years.

His stomach growled loudly, reminding him that he was hungry for more than just James. There would be many other occasions to suck cock. He could do it on the way back home in the carriage if the trip was long enough. As he reluctantly pulled off, he glanced up.

James watched him, eyes wide, bottom lip caught between his teeth. "You're very good."

He got to his feet, caressing James one last time. "I love your cock."

A tiny line grew between James' eyebrows and then disappeared. "I'm glad."

"You can feed yourself to me after we've had our meal. Consider your seed my dessert." Rafe grinned and strolled back into the dressing room to select what he needed. "Are you coming?"

"God, I hope so," James muttered softly, causing Rafe to laugh.

He redressed quickly then played valet for James who appeared all thumbs when it came to his cravat. "Months in the country and you cannot even get dressed as a gentleman should."

"It's you. All I can think about is fucking you."

Now that was good to know. "Eat first, then fuck me. There is plenty of time to do what we want."

CHAPTER EIGHT

We're still friends. After a hearty beefsteak and ale, James followed Rafe into the pit of the Theatre Royal and nodded to acquaintances he passed. His mind was churning with worry now. So far, no one suspected anything was different about him or about Rafe. They didn't have a clue how he felt deep inside. Relief was giving way to intense curiosity. Rafe was taking the situation and change in his inclinations rather well. He had worn a smile almost every moment since their last kiss. It was as if he was as relieved as James.

A stranger hailed Rafe and drew him away a few steps. James watched them together, saw his friend whisper into the man's ear and receive a nod at whatever confidence passed between them. It was a scene James had viewed many times in the past. Rafe had always had other friends who he was not acquainted with, but tonight his curiosity was stirred enough to find out what exactly Rafe talked about.

As he approached, the other man cast a nervous glance in his direction. He seemed familiar, though James couldn't place him. Rafe turned, grinning like a fiend. The same man he'd always known, but it startled him to think that Rafe might have more secrets he'd not shared. It had not been lost on him that his friend appeared at ease when kissed by a man. He drew closer and glanced beyond Rafe's shoulder, just in time to see the other man disappear through the doorway. "What was that about?"

He shrugged. "Are you not interested in the farce tonight?"

James glanced at the performers. On stage, a woman shrieked a fearful note and the crowd around them booed and hissed. He turned back. "Maybe not."

"Would you rather go somewhere else, a tavern or

another theatre or simply call it a night?"

He nodded. "Let's go home."

What he wanted was to go somewhere to talk about what they'd done together and what it meant for their friendship and a possible future for him. He had never made plans to let alone be intimate with Rafe. He'd intended to kiss a stranger, bugger one too, before he died. To be intimate with someone he held no strong ties with. The way he felt about Rafe significantly complicated his decision.

Rafe led the way back out and strolled the halls toward the main exit. Two tall figures blocked their way, one a human island that every other gentleman had to skirt around. The Duke of Staines was known to James but only by reputation. They did not move in the same circles and he had not been graced with the same invitation to join the Hunt Club as Rafe had received.

The other man, a tall unremarkable gentleman, he wasn't acquainted with.

Irritation filled him anew that Rafe had a membership to the exclusive club he wouldn't elaborate on, so he made to move past them without speaking a word.

Rafe however, stopped. "Good evening, Your Grace."

James paused, wishing they could just go straight home to his bed.

"Ah, Lord Raphael, and is that Lord Claymore I see hovering at your side? Very brave of you to explore the pit." The duke looked them over, an inspection that made James feel ten years old and very, very guilty. "Lord Claymore. A pleasure to see you again."

He had little choice but to shake the man's outstretched hand. "Your Grace."

"Did you not find the performance to your liking this evening?"

Rafe grinned. "I'd rather hear Marinari sing again."

James frowned, not knowing who they referred to but assumed it was someone from the Hunt Club. The stranger chuckled and then quickly stifled the sound.

"I wouldn't count it a pleasure." The duke's gaze grew intense and then he smiled. "Come to dine tomorrow night. Bring Claymore as a fourth. It's been too long since we've spoken and I'm starved for news of Sussex. Would ten o'clock suit?"

Rafe nodded eagerly, but James wasn't so sure it was a good idea. He had never spoken to the duke much before. Gaining an invitation to a private dinner was an unexpected surprise.

As the two gentlemen moved off, James touched Rafe's sleeve. "I wasn't aware you were so well known to the Duke of Staines, but who was the other gentleman?"

"Redding. The duke's servant and companion. A more loyal shadow you will never see, but who barely says a word, although I do catch him hiding his amusement quite often." Rafe gestured toward the exit. As they stepped outside to wait on their carriage, he began talking again. "You'll like the duke. He's always concerned that everyone is comfortable at the club."

James pushed down his resentment when it flared again. It wasn't Rafe's fault that he'd not been worthy of the coveted invitation. Many gentlemen were not, and it had tempered his enjoyment of London. They'd always done everything else together before Rafe's membership had begun.

Once inside the carriage, Rafe's leg brushed his restlessly as he jiggled it up and down. James hadn't seen the nervous gesture since their first year at school. He slid his hand over Rafe's leg to stop him and they traveled in that fashion for a few moments. It was pleasant to touch him. As he considered the change to their friendship he had to admit he was relieved that Rafe had been the man he'd been with the first time.

When they rounded the next corner, Rafe slipped off the bench and brazenly cupped James' balls through his trousers. James sucked in a sharp breath and then moaned as Rafe teased the tip of his swelling cock with his thumb. "Now, where were we?" he murmured.

He stared at Rafe's mouth a long moment before lifting a finger to his lips and brushed the tip across the plump firm skin of his bottom lip. It was startling to have Rafe touch him, but he could adapt, and adapt quickly he would. "You had me here."

Rafe slid James' finger into his mouth and sucked. The gesture was so arousing that James' balls drew up and he moaned, besotted anew with Rafe and what they might do together.

After a moment, his friend grinned and slowly drew back, licking his lips in a suggestive manner.

James stared at the glistening plump lips and his pulse sped. If not for the carriage, and fear of discovery, he'd be more than happy to continue in this vein. But he had to protect Rafe and that meant maintaining control of his desires until they were safely within the privacy of his home.

He leaned into the corner of the carriage for support. "Better not start."

"Why? Afraid you'll be overcome with lust and someone will catch us in the carriage?"

He nodded. "I am very afraid of losing you."

"You couldn't lose me if you tried." Rafe shoved his hair back from his eyes and impishly grinned. "I would always find you."

The carriage pulled up in front of James' house and Rafe quickly exited, holding the door open and swinging his hand wide in invitation in the place of a servant. James climbed out more slowly, irritated by Rafe's obvious unconcern for his reputation, health and well-being. What they had begun held danger. If anyone found them out, more than one life would be ruined. They each had families to protect from gossip.

He let himself into the dark townhouse and locked the door behind them. He studied Rafe, overcome by conflicting feelings. Desire surely, but his anxiety had returned. He'd made a plan and he always stuck by them. He'd meant to carry them out in secret so no one would know his shame, yet Rafe was now intimately tied to his downfall. Would he understand what drove him toward his final goal? Would he forgive him for taking his own life rather than face what society condemned as an unacceptable desire for men?

James led the way upstairs into the quiet darkness,

his heart heavy.

Rafe caught his hand after a few steps and squeezed. "You had a question earlier that you did not ask."

Having his hand held by a man was rather odd, but James found it pleasant to hold Rafe's. He threaded their fingers together and held on tightly. "Is that so?"

"You get that funny little crinkle in your brow and then it went away." Rafe gestured between his eyes.

James reached his room and then stood still. "You know me so well."

Rafe tugged him 'round to face him. "There is always more to learn. Ask?"

"You've been buggered before?"

His friend nodded. His eyes, when they rose, hid nothing. "I have. I am no stranger to a man's bed."

A strange sensation grew in James's chest. "You've a lover now?"

"I've never been seriously involved with anyone."

Although his tension eased somewhat, bitterness filled James and he turned away. "Yet the act is serious."

"With you, I agree it is. I never imagined you'd want me."

He sank into a chair. "I never imagined it either. Not until recent events."

Rafe moved closer a few steps. "Something happened?"

"Something didn't." He shook his head. The only way he'd gotten a rise with a woman was to keep his eyes firmly closed and imagine he wasn't with her. His most useful fantasy had featured men, only occasionally had he allowed himself to think of Rafe and only if he'd been in danger of failing. He'd felt so ashamed about that. Those desires were not normal and he'd concluded but one path open to him. "I..."

"No, you don't have to explain the details as I can see it troubles you still," Rafe said quickly, holding up a hand. "I've never cared to hear about your women and if you've a taste for our own sex then it's not unexpected."

James stared. "That's a surprise. You always asked."

"Had to." Rafe tangled his fingers through his hair. "Never wanted you to suspect me of preferring the backdoor to the front. Bloody hard to hide anything from you at the best of times."

His friend didn't know how good he was. James would never have expected him to enjoy being fucked or sucking cock or even kissing men. "What do we do?"

Rafe came closer, widened his legs over James' and straddled him. His fingers tangled in James' hair. A smile tugged his lips as he settled himself comfortably. As with anything new, the position felt odd for barely a moment. He kissed him and looped his arms about James' shoulders. "I imagine nothing else need change but this, what we do together while alone. We have always been close friends, visiting each other's homes often. No one will suspect our inclinations are somewhat more carnal."

James slid his hands up Rafe's thighs, remembering the warmth and firm skin beneath. "Is that what you want, to go on as usual?"

"Well, a little more cock would make me happy. Next time you go down to Sussex do you think I might be worthy of an invitation to stay a while?"

"Of course." The idea of having Rafe near at Claymore was both arousing and a little frightening. They would have to be bloody careful. There was dense pocket of forest he usually skirted when riding, but deep inside was a clearing and a very soft patch of grass perfect for amorous adventures. "What do we do in Town?"

Rafe eased James' coat from his shoulders, waistcoat from his chest and then loosened his cravat. "We spend as much time together as we can, every chance we get to touch, we take it. I really did miss you." His fingers caught his shirt and tugged. The tightness of his trousers proved a hindrance at first and after a brief battle, James lost his shirt too. The warmth of Rafe's hands skimming over his chest was arousing. His friend combed his fingers through James's chest hair, scraped his nails lightly over his nipples, an unfocussed expression on his face. Rafe curled his fingers around James's upper arm. The look in his eyes hinted he liked what he saw and touched. "Have you done all the work at Claymore yourself?"

"Some," James murmured, as he went to work on Rafe's clothes. "I find great satisfaction in using my hands."

"Use them now on me." Rafe kissed him hard and after an initial struggle for dominance, James ended up on top of Rafe on the hardwood floor, his cock pressing inside his friend once more and both of them laughing over Rafe's futile struggles to free himself.

CHAPTER NINE

After a brief return home to change clothes, check on his father's health and spar with his stepmother over his recent absence, Rafe stepped into the Duke of Staines's residence with excitement filling him. Tonight he would dine with James before a man who would overlook any covert touches between them.

He'd been reluctant to leave James at all, but he couldn't wear borrowed clothes all day, and certainly not to dinner with a very observant man. He forced himself to relax as he accepted a drink from the Duke of Staines' companion. "Thank you, Redding."

Polite to a fault, the man nodded, and moved to the side of the room, slightly out of the way but still close enough to hear every word. The Duke of Staines leaned forward. "You seem unaccountably happy. Happier than I've seen you in a long time, Lord Raphael."

Rafe sipped his drink and chose his words with care. "I'm happy for the invitation to dinner and the chance for pleasant company."

"That's quite all right." The duke shifted in his chair. "I've been meaning to speak to you privately away from the club. I have heard the odd whisper about your father's failing health and I'm growing concerned. How is he today?"

Unsurprised by the duke's knowledge, he sighed. "Much the same. My stepmother has finally brought a physician to him, and a bloodletting has been done, though from what I've learned there seems little hope of a fast improvement."

The duke looked over at Redding. "Find out what you can and report to Lord Raphael tomorrow."

Redding nodded. "First thing tomorrow?"

"A ride first and then I'll let you go." The duke faced Rafe. "Redding has a keen interest in the physic of the sick and is well-versed in treatments that don't require further bloodletting. If he cannot detect the cause then he may choose to consult with an acquaintance of some renown. Is that acceptable?"

"It is very generous of you both to take an interest." Rafe let out a deep breath. "I must confess I know little of illness except to avoid my father when he's suffering from one."

Redding nodded, attention flickering to the duke. "Most ordinary men are difficult to manage at the best of times. A lord who is unwell is quite another matter."

The duke roared with laughter. "Redding is too modest by half. He's quite skilled. Saved my life more than once."

Redding's brow rose as he looked to the duke. "I trust those days are behind us."

The duke winked. "Of course, I've no inclination for mischief any longer. Trust me."

"One day." Redding grinned and then wiped the expression clear again. "Excuse me. There is a matter I must attend to." Redding strolled out and spoke to the butler outside.

"I don't know what I'd do without him," the duke confided.

Rafe set his glass aside and cast a surreptitious glance toward the clock. James was running late. "He seems very efficient."

"He likes to fuss. And I let him. Makes for a harmonious household. At my age, I'm coming to prefer simplicity in my living arrangements. He's become a close friend and will dine with us tonight."

He gaped. A servant dining with his master? How distinctly odd. And yet it had not escaped his notice that a change had come over the duke in recent months. Although he'd been away for a few of them at his estate, he'd returned to London a contented man, though he still fussed over the club members. As Redding returned, and the duke's eyes lit with unmistakable warmth, Rafe began to entertain a suspicion about the relationship between the duke and his servant.

Redding smiled softly. "Lord Claymore's carriage has

just drawn up."

"Excellent." The duke smiled. "I'm looking forward to getting to know Claymore better. His father was an unmitigated bore, and I hope I misjudged the son."

"You certainly have," Rafe asserted quickly. Was there a chance the duke might invite James into the club? "Claymore is a man of honor and enjoys a good laugh."

If James joined the club they might enjoy the club's secrecy and make love there without fear of discovery. Many lords conducted their affairs with other lords within those walls. The only drawback to that arrangement was that James might not only choose to be with him every time. Access to unfettered pleasure could corrupt even the gentlest soul. Claymore was not particularly timid when it came to most matters. How would he feel if given the opportunity to make love to a vast array of men? The idea unsettled Rafe enough that his palms grew damp. He did not want to share James with anyone.

When James strode in to greet the duke, Rafe pushed aside his unsettled thoughts and schooled his features to hide his happiness. The man took his breath away on a normal day, and after making love to him, he was afraid his feelings were writ large on his face. After a few minutes of anxious observation it seemed the two were off to a great start.

"Rafe was just telling me about the improvements you've made at Claymore. How goes the work?"

James settled into a chair near Rafe. "Fine. Fine. The house is in much better condition than when I inherited it but there is still much to be done."

"You must be anxious to return to the work or do you have a competent steward?"

"I had a vacancy but found good help at last."

"As you have several vacancies in your townhouse too." The duke glanced between them. "It's a little empty, isn't it?

"It is." James shifted in his seat. "I wanted to make some changes this Season."

"Are those changes still underway at home or has the

place seemed a little fuller since Lord Raphael stopped by and never left?" The duke smirked. "I do wonder what keeps him there at all hours of the day and night. Must be a rather demanding guest."

Rafe sucked in a sharp breath at the subtle innuendo implicit in the duke's words and he kept his gaze away from James. But somehow he suspected the duke had guessed about the change in their friendship. He and James had not had a chance to talk about how other men of their inclinations handled remarks about the company they kept. At the club it was an open secret if one liked cock or cunny or both. Here though, James might feel threatened since he did not know about the duke or the club's secret activities.

Redding stepped forward and touched the duke's shoulder. "Ambrose."

The duke glanced up and for a moment, Rafe imagined the duke looked a little abashed. He smiled benignly and patted the hand resting on his shoulder. "Forgive me. I am forever meddling in other people's affairs."

"And he's not joking either," Redding murmured softly.

The duke merely laughed and stood. "Shall we go into dinner? I promise no more ill-timed questions."

Rafe nodded and turned to James, whose face had pinked. He moved to James's side and softly touched his back. His friend stiffened, but when the duke and Redding were a few steps away, he nodded, drew a deep breath and gestured for Rafe to lead on.

The duke and Redding preceded them into a large dining room, containing a mahogany table twice as long as it was broad. As they crossed into the room, the duke captured Redding's hand briefly before they parted company to sit at opposite sides of the table.

Rafe stopped in his tracks. The duke and his servant *were* lovers? He'd never suspected them to have gone so far but...

James stopped at his side too and Rafe quickly turned to him to see if he'd noticed. His eyes had widened and he asked without words whether Rafe had noticed the touch.

He nodded. Such a relationship wasn't unheard of between servant and master. He doubted many were openly shown, and who was he to quibble about where a duke might place his heart. From all he'd seen, Redding was devoted to the duke and the duke always had Redding somewhere close at hand. They were always together now he thought of it further which made an affair between them very clever.

Rafe tipped his head to move James along into dinner. They were as fortunate as the duke to have a close friendship in their lives. Now they could be even closer. He wanted to share everything. The good and the bad.

CHAPTER TEN

James rubbed his hips against Rafe, excited beyond belief by how the evening had ended. Dinner with the Duke of Staines had even been pleasant when he'd expected to feel an outsider. There had been no further talk about the Hunt Club during the evening and for that he was both relieved and curious. What exactly did Rafe do at the club for so many hours at a time?

He buried his face against Rafe's throat as the front door of his empty home was closed and the world locked out. He inhaled the addictive scent of his lover and his need rose. He had never imagined Rafe would rouse such impatience in him, but he was unable to stop touching his long limbs and warm skin. He nibble on his jaw to elicit a reaction. "What are you thinking about?"

"Tomorrow and the days after that."

A wave of guilt swept over him. He'd made no plans beyond the date of his birth. He'd planned to end his life than rather live as a sodomite. Now though ...

James straightened away from Rafe. What could he do now?

He'd be blind to miss that all was not normal between the Duke of Staines and the servant, Redding. Since when do dukes share their meals with a servant anyway? He'd never heard of it done until tonight unless it was during travel. The duke conversed with Redding as equals and he strongly suspected they were lovers.

Rafe shook his head from side to side. "I have to return home soon. A while back I made a devil's bargain to take at least one meal a day with my father. Having missed one he will become surly about any further lapses."

James knew all about bargains, even when they were with one's self. "What deal did you make?"

His friend tightly curled his arms around James'

waist. "That he would cease harping on about me taking a wife and learning the family business of yields and rents."

"Ah," James' stomach lurched in dread. "You should go home then."

"I will," Rafe leaned close, "but not until the sun is about to rise and we've ridden long and hard."

A wave of warmth crept over his face and body. There was nothing more he wanted than to spend every moment of every day in Rafe's company, but that wasn't possible. "I've no horses to ride."

Rafe laughed softly. "Then ride me. For miles if you've the stamina for it."

James opened his mouth at the taunting then realized that Rafe was both teasing and daring him at the same time. He pinned his lover to the hall wall with the weight of his body. "You doubt me?"

Rafe quickly kissed him, tangling tongues in a way that provoked James beyond belief. "I won't when I have proof."

Despite the desire inflaming him, James couldn't help but laugh. "I thought things would be different."

"Not a chance." Rafe touched his face, scraping his fingernails over his jaw. "I will always be foolish enough to make you smile and laugh at me. You were looking a bit too grim again, my friend."

He caught Rafe's hip and squeezed. "Rafe?"

"Hmm hmm."

"You could have given me a hint before this to soften the surprise."

Rafe shook his head. "Thought about it many times, but then our conversation turned to women and I didn't dare. Why didn't you tell me?"

James sobered. "How could I tell you what I was never sure about? I'm sure now and its changed things for me in a way I never considered. I missed you more than I let on while I was in the country."

The other man's shoulders rose and fell as he gulped in air. "I missed you, too," he whispered. "So damn much and I couldn't even tell you why." He went to work on the fastenings of his clothes and before too long, a puddle of fabric lay about them.

James gripped the back of Rafe's head in one hand. "Well, I had suspected you might have missed my company. Your letters seemed to indicate a certain level of misery."

He ducked the slow punch Rafe swung at him, laughing at his friend and never happier. When Rafe took off up the stairs with his clothes waving about as trophies, James chased him. He tackled him onto the bed and they wrestled for a few moments, hands sliding everywhere. He liked this side of making love to a man. He didn't have to curb his strength as he would with a woman in his bed. He allowed Rafe to flip him onto his back and straddle his thighs.

Having Rafe, hovering over him, caused his cock to thicken. His friend wriggled closer, sitting over his hips, settling his balls over his groin. All the blood in James' body quickly rushed south. He sat up, slid his hands up Rafe's torso and claimed another kiss. "Bloody tease."

Then, before Rafe could resist, he flipped them over, forcing the other man flat on his back and covered him. Slowly, he rubbed himself against his best friend.

"Bloody bossy bastard," Rafe complained, but since he was laughing the next moment James did not take him seriously.

He worked a hand between them and cupped his hand over Rafe's groin. The feel was extraordinary. His hand was full of heat, hardness, a clear sign of how aroused his friend was by what they did together. He shifted so he could get a better grip through the garment and Rafe's back arched as he pushed his cock against James's hand. "That feels so good."

"I hope so. Never done this before."

Rafe's eyes widened. "Never?"

"Never. But I'm a quick learner." He leaned on one arm and continued to rub the bulge beneath the breeches, watching Rafe's face for signs he was doing it right.

His lover groaned and writhed on the bed. After a moment, James stopped, lowered his gaze to Rafe's groin and worked the first button free. Rafe sucked his stomach in and James lowered his mouth to kiss it. He shifted so he could use both hands and exposed Rafe's cock to his gaze. The hard length made his mouth water, and determined to please him, he kissed the tip. The salty seed on his tongue made his cock ache as it never had before. He licked the ruddy head with long sweeps of his tongue. He experimented, guided by Rafe's response and what he'd enjoyed himself.

When he'd licked from root to tip, he took the whole length into his mouth as far as he could. Damned if he could match Rafe's skill for depth, but he did his best.

Rafe clawed at his hair. "God, you're beautiful like that."

Rather than answer, James continued to bob on his length learning what it took to please his lover. When his grunts and moans grew to fever pitch, he pulled off and dragged Rafe's breeches completely off his legs.

Rafe was on his knees the next second, his hands on the buttons of James' breeches. He opened them slowly, fingertips brushing the head of his cock.

James moaned at the touch and when Rafe wrapped his hand around him and stroked with a firm grip, he almost lost it then and there. "Jesus."

His lover was brutal, overloading James' senses so quickly that seed dripped from the tip in a steady stream. Rafe lowered his head and took him deep into his mouth on the first attempt.

James ripped his head away before he came down his throat. "Please. Stop."

The grin Rafe threw at him was one of utter bliss. He fell onto his back with a contented sigh, knees raised. "It's good for you that I like bossy men."

The sight of Rafe making himself comfortable caused his heart to tumble over. He'd never had a friend so dear to him. It was almost as if . . . James shook his head to dispel the shocking idea and instead threw himself on Rafe. They tussled again but, since neither had trousers on, the sensations were completely pleasurable. Their cocks rubbed together and the desire that filled him was so incredible that he looked down at what they did.

Rafe threaded his fingers through James' hair to lift his gaze. "Like that do you?"

"Yes." He liked everything about Rafe and their time together. Whether it was a day at the races, suffering through a ball, or sucking cock, James couldn't wish for a better companion. He and Rafe matched.

His friend planted his feet on the bed and widened his thighs so James could fit his hips between. Although he had no idea how they could fuck in this position he was willing to bet Rafe would guide him if it became necessary.

When Rafe drew his knees toward his chest James' cock slid lower between parted cheeks. He stilled, uncertain of what came next.

"Come up on your knees, Jimmy. Hold my legs as high up as you need."

He did as Rafe asked, noticing immediately that his lover's tight puckered arse was more exposed in this position. James swallowed, overcome by absolute certainty that he wanted this for the rest of his life, no matter how short it might be. With seed running down his length he was desperate for Rafe. He didn't want to hurt Rafe and glanced around for Rafe's flask to ease the way.

The other man was already one step ahead and handed it over. "Hurry."

"You're sure I won't hurt you? It was only yesterday that I... I thought it would be painful."

Rafe nodded. "It's not like I've not taken a man before."

Although he knew it, James took a long moment to absorb the reminder. Anger simmered at the obvious conclusion that Rafe had been taken so often that he was well used to a rough fuck and the experience was commonplace. He didn't like the idea one little bit. His jealousy fired his blood and he took himself in hand, guiding his head to his friend's arse to claim what was his.

The sensation as he pushed against the ring was still so different he gasped aloud. Rafe gently touched his arms. "I'm yours now. Work yourself in a bit at a time."

James pressed in, discovering how good fucking a man in this position could be compared to his past experience with women. That difference excited him more. He did as Rafe bid, thrusting carefully and retreating until he was firmly lodged. When his balls touched Rafe, he finally met his lover's eyes.

His friend grinned. "Fuck me."

He drew back and, watching Rafe's face, he slowly made love. After a time, Rafe's squirming increased, he clutched at James. His breathing growing labored. James increased his pace, loving this. Loving Rafe.

He stilled. Caught up in the discovery. He was in love at long last.

He loved his best friend. Wonder filled him. *After all this time.*

"God, James, don't stop now. Don't stop," Rafe groaned as he took himself in hand. He pumped his cock and James matched his movements, thrusting in time, as they often did everything.

Rafe groaned suddenly, shuddering violently beneath and around him, pale seed landing on his smooth chest. The clench of muscle around his cock caught James by surprise. He lasted two more thrusts before he shot his seed inside his friend. He couldn't hold back the shout of joy and after a few more thrusts, collapsed on top of Rafe. He lay panting, sweaty and satisfied with Rafe holding him close. He didn't worry about crushing him or needing to move. If he grew too heavy, Rafe was strong enough to toss him off and maybe they'd make love again.

CHAPTER ELEVEN

Rafe peeked over the rim of his coffee cup, now cooled to almost artic temperatures, and worried for his father. A sheen of sweat coated the Earl of Norwich's brow and upper lip. Eating barely a quarter of his usual breakfast shouldn't exhaust him. He chose his next words with care. "Father, Claymore indicated he hoped to call on you. Are you busy today?"

What he really wanted to ask was if his father was well enough to see anyone.

"Naturally, I am very busy, but not too busy to see Lord Claymore."

The fiction his father liked to persist in amused him no longer. He'd picked at his food today and when Rafe had questioned his father's valet, he'd been alarmed to discover his father had trouble keeping down any food at all. "He said he'd call at eleven."

His father cast a startled glance at the clock. The hands showed it was almost that hour now. The meal and getting his father to eat anything had taken far longer than usual. Rafe had thought to be finished and downstairs in the drawing room, ready to greet Claymore with a welcoming smile and reassurance that no one could tell he'd been fucked so well he could still feel it.

But his father made no move to rise from bed and Rafe didn't dare leave his side.

Although knowing affection of any sort would be wasted on his sire, he patted his foot where it rested beneath the bedding. "Claymore will not care you are not risen yet."

His father snorted, a frown growing on his brow. "Then I will not put myself out for his amusement. He should have called on us far sooner than this. When he first came up to Town in fact."

He glanced at the barely touched plate then stole a

cold slice of ham from it, gobbling it down quickly so his stepmother would not suspect Father of eating so little. Her fussing put his teeth on edge and made his father cranky. She was due to return any moment and Rafe would rather not endure her lectures again. "Well, he'll be here soon."

His father pushed the tray toward him and Rafe finished the plate. When he was done he took it to the door where Norwich's valet lingered, eavesdropping as the man was encouraged to do at every turn by his stepmother. As he handed the tray over, he heard the knocker echo through the house. Thinking it might be Jimmy, he turned back to his father to warn him only to see him reach for the chamber pot and cast up his accounts.

The valet dropped the tray onto the floor where they stood and rushed to his father's side, curling a supportive arm around his back and holding out a napkin. Rafe stared in shock as his father continued to retch in the most hideous way while clutching at his stomach as if he were in great pain. His own stomach clenched. Rafe clamped his hand over his mouth to keep his breakfast down.

When Norwich was done, he collapsed onto the bed, sweating and moaning in misery as the valet fussed.

His father was far more ill than anyone had let on. Rafe's heart began to beat fast and hard. His stepmother had deliberately withheld the news.

The butler approached. "Lord Claymore is here to see Lord Norwich."

Rafe glanced at his father then headed downstairs to delay the meeting. His father was too sick for visitors. Jimmy waited in the drawing room and smiled when he entered. Rafe crossed to his side immediately. "My father cannot see you today."

James glanced up. "I'm sorry to hear that."

"He needs help." He shook his head. He'd barely been sick a day in his life. "I don't understand why I wasn't informed he was so bad, but I intend to have him seen by someone I trust. Someone from the club."

"That Redding chap?"

He nodded. "I'll start there. The duke places great faith in him."

"I've nothing else to do today, so if you don't mind I'd like to accompany you."

Rafe glanced at the clock on the mantle. "They'll be at the club. Only members are allowed inside."

James didn't even blink or speak a word of protest that he had, again, to be excluded. "Then I will wait in the carriage while you seek them inside. Come. Time is of the essence. My carriage shouldn't have gone far and can take us there quickly."

Relief filled him. "Thank you."

His friend led the way, as he was prone to do, and before too much time had passed they were drawn up before the Hunt Club's entrance way. Rafe felt a little guilty about leaving Jimmy behind, but there was nothing he could do about the matter. Invitations to the club were out of his hands. All he could do was hope that one day James might be included. He tapped on the door to a small room the duke kept for his personal use and shuffled his feet until answered.

Redding poked his head out. "Yes?"

"My father. I need you to see him. I fear he's gravely ill."

The door opened further and the duke appeared, stripped down to his waistcoat. "I thought it was a trifling matter."

"He vomited this morning. Even I know that is not good."

Redding pushed past him. "I'll get my bag and send for Richards too."

The Duke of Staines retrieved his coat and shrugged into it. "Take us there."

"Thank you, but there is no need to stir yourself." Rafe wiped the sweat from his brow. "Claymore is waiting with his carriage outside."

"Claymore, eh?" His eyes softened. "I'd rather accompany Redding if you don't mind. Ladies tend to have a different view of a servant attending their titled husbands, even when they know what they are doing. We will be there shortly, I promise, if you'd like to return to Claymore with the news that we will be joining you both."

"Thank you." Rafe returned to the carriage and when he reached it he collapsed onto the bench beside James. He rubbed a hand over his belly as a stitch formed. "They'll be here in a moment."

"That's good news."

"It is." Rafe wiped his brow with the back of his hand. "Open a window, would you. It's sweltering in here."

Jimmy opened the window and then faced him, his brow creased with concern. "It really isn't so warm as you imagine. You're just worrying over your father. I'm sure its nothing." He caressed Rafe's thigh until the duke and Redding arrived. The newcomers greeted Jimmy, and Rafe was questioned about what he knew of his father's illness. "Never suspected it was so serious."

Redding peeked into his bag, frowning at the contents. "It could be many things. A disease, bad food, a poisoning. It's hard to say without seeing him and hearing all the details. You say you've not seen much of him."

Rafe shrugged. His stomach continued to cramp uncomfortably. "He's a hard man to be around for any extended length of time."

The carriage turned a corner as Redding agreed that many fathers were the same, no matter their class or background. Rafe gripped the edge of the seat as another cramp ripped through him. Another corner and he knew all hope was lost to keep his last meal down. He thumped the roof of the carriage to make the coachman stop, opened the door before the carriage had come to a complete halt and launched himself out. He made it to an alley beside a grand house before his breakfast reappeared. He hunched over as he retched and retched, only vaguely aware Jimmy had followed and was holding him up from the ground.

When he finally stopped, he felt as weak as a newborn kitten. Jimmy half-carried him back to the carriage and propped him against the corner of the bench seat. "So sorry," he managed to choke out.

"Don't be." His friend dabbed at his brow with his own handkerchief. "I thought you were well again."

The duke's gaze narrowed on them. "Has Lord Raphael been ill too?"

The carriage resumed its journey and Rafe closed his eyes before answering. "Too much to drink, too quickly perhaps."

"The day I returned I thought him pale and thinner than I remember," Jimmy clarified, filling in the specifics quickly. "He's been entirely well since that first day, so I thought his apathy only on account of his poor appetite and lack of sleep."

Rafe opened his eyes as his stomach cramped again. "Wasn't hungry because of the nausea. That came first."

Redding leaned forward, eyes narrowed. "What did you do last night?"

"Nothing. I was with the duke and then returned to James' townhouse."

"Hmm, and this morning? You've spent the whole of it together."

"No. Rafe left me early and returned home to Norwich." Jimmy squeezed his hand. "Did you have breakfast with your father before your concerns for him changed to alarm?"

He clung to James' hand like it was his only lifeline as another bout of cramps grew in strength. "Yes, he picked at his food then cast up what he'd eaten."

"How much did you eat?"

"Everything sent up," Rafe's eyes widened. "Then I ate what my father hadn't managed, so he'd be spared my stepmother's fussing."

"Dear God," Redding whispered in shock.

The duke set a hand to Redding's shoulder. "What is it?"

"My suspicions might be wrong," Redding said quickly, his brow furrowing.

Jimmy pulled Rafe into his arms and held him close. "He's thinking its poison but won't say so. Rafe, I am afraid I suspect the same. You only became ill when you went home. Is it always the case?"

"Not always." Rafe swallowed as the sensation of nausea struck him anew. It couldn't be poison. "Not like this."

"Do you often eat from your father's plate?" The duke asked in a quiet, determined voice that made the hair on the back of Rafe's neck stand up.

"No," he whispered with a sinking heart. "Today was the first, and the first time sickness has struck me so great a blow."

The duke nodded and then glanced at his companion. "Be cautious at first, Red. No accusations until you are certain the source has been found. Consult with Richards quietly, but do it quickly."

Redding nodded, his gaze focused on the window. "Richards will surely come quickly and I'll allow him to come to his own conclusions before voicing any suspicions we might have."

Rafe settled into Jimmy's arms, little caring that he looked a damned, besotted fool. If not for his friend's presence he'd be facing this situation alone. The warmth pressing against his right side drove the awful chill from his blood. Was someone trying to kill his father, and likely him as well? But why?

When they arrived at Norwich house and faced his father, Jimmy was by his side every moment, offering silent support as Redding questioned the earl about his symptoms. Rafe was questioned again too, and he left no complaint from the telling. He discovered he and his father had remarkably similar symptoms, though his father's were more severe.

Once the examinations were complete, his father waved for him to come to him and Rafe caught the trembling hand he held out. "You never let on you were ill."

"I never thought it important enough to mention. You might have insisted I stay home."

His father's pale cheeks pinked. "I would have and then you might have become more ill."

Rather disconcerted by the fear weakening his father's

voice, he turned his face away, gaze falling on the side table where a jar of peppermints sat. He scowled. "You've had your valet sneak into my room again. Those are mine."

Father huffed. "They were your mother's first. The scent reminds me of her many kindnesses."

"She loved just to sniff them." Rafe lifted the squat jar that usually sat on his writing desk and since he had none in his pockets now, opened the jar and popped one in his mouth.

"Stop," Jimmy ordered loudly, then before he could act, Jimmy grabbed his jaw, pried open his mouth and dug the sweet out with his big fingers before he'd barely sucked on it. He held up the wet blob. "Don't eat another thing from the kitchens of this house unless you want to risk becoming ill again."

Rafe looked at him in puzzlement. "My mother made those."

James shook his head and tossed the sweet into the fire. "She did not make this particular one, did she?"

Rafe's mother had died a long time ago. Cook made them now at his request. "No. I suppose not."

James took the jar and handed it over to Redding, and then started to empty Rafe's pockets onto the bed. "Rafe has eaten these since he was a boy. Always has a dozen in his pocket."

While he didn't mind Jimmy pawing at his clothes, his behavior wouldn't gain him anything. Rafe pushed his hands away. "There's none to be found on me today. The tin was empty and I left it beside the bed."

Jimmy's eyes narrowed and then he nodded. "Everyone in this house knows how fond Lord Raphael is of the sweets."

Redding sniffed at the contents then went to confer with the other physician in quiet voices on the far side of the room. James pushed Rafe into a chair close to the bed and took a place beside it. After a time, Redding called the duke over to their corner. When Staines nodded, turned with a decisive movement and stared at Norwich with pity-filled eyes, Rafe could only conclude the prognosis was exactly as they had feared.

"Poison it is. Likely inheritance powder, arsenic, or something worse." The duke's expression hardened into one of fury, the likes of which Rafe had never encountered before at the club. "Search the house at once. I want everyone questioned, every jar investigated and the contents confirmed. Lord Norwich, I would like to offer my aid to investigate and until the culprit is detained and brought to justice I invite you to repair to my residence until your health is restored."

Norwich sat up a little straighter. The duke did not invite outsiders, those not connected to his club, into his home often. "Of course. I'll send for my wife and second son."

"I would not advise it." The duke shook his head. "In matters such as these I feel the best solution is to separate the ill from the healthy. Lord Raphael can recuperate under Lord Claymore's watchful eye if he is agreeable. I would like no further opportunities for mischief to present themselves for yourself and your heir."

When his father's eyes widened, Rafe knew exactly what the duke and his father had realized. The one who stood to gain the most from the death of Norwich and his heir was the spare. His brother Ian.

He sank back into the chair shock, his heart crushed. He couldn't believe it of Ian at first, but the outcome, if their supposed illness had continued unchecked, would have made his brother the next earl. Bile burned the back of his throat and he pressed a hand to his cramping stomach.

Jimmy, after a brief consultation with the duke and Redding, took Rafe from Norwich house and into the safety of his care.

CHAPTER TWELVE

James pulled Rafe into his arms and held him. Worry and relief filled his mind. For the moment, his friend was safe. But he couldn't help but think of tomorrow. What if he'd not been here? Tomorrow was supposed to be his last day on earth not Rafe's. "Is it all right to hold you like this?"

Rafe patted his hand and then squeezed. "Yes."

He sighed. The shock of almost losing Rafe, as he would assuredly had done if he'd stayed away from London even longer, resurfaced. He didn't know who had made the attempt on Norwich's life, but he had a strong idea why. Power, money, position. More than likely it was for the money.

"I've spoiled your plans, haven't I?" Rafe snuggled against him. "Do you still have time to do all you need to do before you return to Sussex?"

James did not want to lie to Rafe anymore. He wanted to be honest about his despair and his uncertainty about the future. Even more so now when it seemed there was everything to lose. "I wasn't going back to Sussex. I had other intentions for my life."

Rafe wriggled in his arms, his hand skimmed across James's stomach to grip his side. "What were they?"

"Nothing."

Rafe squeezed him and chuckled softly. "I find that hard to believe."

"I wanted to reach my birthday and end my life a happy man."

"At eight and twenty? That's not much of a life," Rafe argued.

James sighed heavily. "Almost all my plans are complete."

Rafe yawned. "What's left to do besides boating?"

"Just the boating."

His friend tensed then he sat up, straddling James so he couldn't move. "What are you talking about? You always have a hundred things to do on your mind at once. It's one of your most endearing and equally frustrating qualities. You make a man think he doesn't think enough."

"You didn't hear me." He brushed his fingertips across Rafe's belly, circling low but avoiding his spent cock. "I was going to end my miserable life."

His friend caught his hand and pinned it to the bed beside his head. "You're in misery now?"

James shook his head and then cupped Rafe's face. "I was truly miserable but no longer. Not since we kissed."

Rafe's eyes narrowed and then he sprang from James' bed. He threw on a shirt and started to pace the room. James sat up slowly and dangled his legs over the side of the bed, watching his friend take in what he'd said and hoping he'd been clear enough at last. When he returned to stand before James, his expression was incredulous. He was too far away to touch but close enough not to miss the hurt on his face. "You have no bloody servants," he growled.

James nodded.

"You extracted a promise from me to look out for your sister when she comes out into Society."

Again he nodded. He'd gotten everything he wanted from Rafe and more.

"You bastard." His friend crossed his arms over his chest. "How dare you think I would live without you?"

Startled by the certainty and impassioned anger in Rafe's voice, James stood and took a pace forward. "I never meant to hurt you, but I need to be honest. I couldn't imagine living like this."

"As my lover."

James shook his head. "I never dreamed you could be mine."

"I've always been yours." Rafe's brows drew together. "When we were boys and since we've been older. I have always considered your opinion first, but you didn't think of mine. How was I supposed to accept your decision?"

"I did think of you. Of everyone. I wanted to protect our friendship and my family. I hadn't planned for you to ever learn I lusted for men."

"For all men? So now you've had me you're moving on to another."

James caught Rafe with both hands and held him steady. "No one else. Just you."

"You blinkered, stubborn fool." Rafe slumped. "There's no need for drastic measures such as you planned. If I'd known from the start how things lay for you then I could have explained how our life could be together and when apart. There is no need for fear if you are careful. Discreet. There are many men in our society that share our inclinations and you'd never even suspect them of any of that when you see them about Town. I don't want to lose you."

Surety made him smile. "You won't. Not now." He pulled Rafe back to the bed and held him tightly against him. "It is still true I have no plans for the future though. My life is a blank page now."

"Sounds like mine has always been. Stumbling from one event to another. Never certain where best to spend my time when I'm not with you. But I know what I want. I want to share my life with you." Rafe lifted his head and smiled shyly. "Care to make your plans with me in mind this time?"

The chill he'd been fighting these past months fled. "I will. I want to."

"Good." Rafe snuggled into his arms and sighed. "Stay in London until this mess with my father is sorted. I'd like to know he was on the mend before we do anything else. I could do with a few weeks or months in the country. You can teach me about sheep and hay. My father would never object to that or consider we might be otherwise engaged too."

James pressed a kiss to the top of Rafe's head. The first time he'd ever done such a thing to a man. Before the gesture would have been an empty show of affection for a woman. Now though, his heart beat just a bit faster at the idea he would never lose the man in his arms. "I doubt I'd need to teach you anything, but I want you at Claymore with me more than anything. I can bear the lie if it protects us. Promise me you will stay away from Ian."

Rafe brushed his lips across James' bare chest. "You know me, I always try to avoid my brother."

CHAPTER THIRTEEN

Avoiding Ian proved rather difficult when they were both woken at the ungodly hour of six by a fierce pounding on the front door. "It could be about my father," Rafe suggested, heart filling swiftly with concern and dread.

Jimmy rose from their bed and pulled on his trousers. "I will discover the truth. Stay here in bed and rest. You are recovering from a botched poisoning, remember."

"I feel better in truth," he admitted, rubbing his hand over his aching body and grasping his cock as the sight of Jimmy's large body filled him with contentment. "A little more attention here would make the world of difference."

"Later." Jimmy scowled, but his gaze strayed to Rafe's swelling cock. "Humor me and stay right there. If it's important, I promise you I will call out."

He wasn't about to risk both their lives by being caught in a compromising position in Jimmy's bed so he scrambled out of the tangled sheets and started dressing in more of James' clothes.

James simply threw on yesterday's breeches and shirt and made his way downstairs barefoot. Rafe hurried to dress so he might not miss anything and when he was respectable enough he moved to the head of the staircase.

Jimmy crept down the stairs and paused at the base. He looked up and pointed. "Your brother," he whispered.

Rafe nodded and moved out of sight. He heard the front door bolts drawn and the creak of the door on his hinges. "Lord Ian. What an unexpected surprise to see you today."

Footsteps boomed in the house. "Where is he? I know he's here."

"Who's here?"

Ian huffed. "Should have known you'd not believe I

had no part in this. I need to speak with my brother. It's urgent."

"Has something happened to Norwich?"

"One could only hope," Ian muttered loud enough that Rafe heard every bitter note. He surged down the steps without thinking of his promise to stay away from Ian. The man had tried to kill his father and him by accident. As soon as he reached his brother he swung his fist, determined to cause him enough pain and suffering to match his own. Ian staggered back, tripped over the bench in the hall and went sprawling across Jimmy's floor in an untidy heap. "Bastard."

Ian looked up, dazed. "What the hell was that for? I'm trying to do you a favor."

Jimmy caught his arm and held him back when he went to strike Ian again. Rafe shook off the grip and glared at his brother. "By acting without honor. By trying to take what should not be yours yet. You disgust me."

"What?" Ian spluttered, wiping at his face with one hand. "I came here to warn you."

"I'm already warned. Now get out of my sight before I really show you what I think of you."

"Well, if that's what you want then I wish you luck." Ian righted himself and collected his hat from where it had fallen in the struggle. He jammed it on his head. "Last time I put myself out to warn him about our father's plans. Enjoy your wife. I hope you'll be very happy together."

Jimmy stepped between them. "What wife?"

Ian grimaced and tugged down his coat. "I don't know why I should bother to tell you, but Norwich is planning a wedding. By month end there'll be a bride at Norwich Park."

Ian attempted to reach the exit, but Jimmy prevented his escape by placing himself against the door. When Ian tried to open it, Jimmy's substantial bodyweight held it shut. "What do you know exactly?"

"I went to see him this morning. Mother mentioned the duke's suspicions about Norwich's illness and confessed he'd been taken away for his health. I went to see him even though warned the duke wasn't likely to let me in as everyone in good health was considered a suspect. I saw him for just a few moments. Father passed a good night. Mama said he would be too ill to see me, but he seemed entirely too happy with his current situation as guest of the Duke of Staines. I thought it odd as Father doesn't care to sleep anywhere but on his own sheets. Father and the duke were deep in conversation when I arrived and the duke remained with him for my short visit. When they left, I clearly heard them agree that marriage was just the thing."

"So?"

"The Duke of Staines has a daughter doesn't he?"

Rafe shook his head. "Not a daughter. He does have a ward who is probably of an age to come out in Society. I've never seen her."

"I don't think anyone has," Jimmy added quietly. "Though rumors abound that her dowry will be quite the prize."

"You will see her if Father has his way." Ian smirked. "Do you think the bargain you made with him will prevent his scheming to make a match for you? He will not be happy until his son has a wife and an heir to bounce on his knee. I'd be more afraid of his silence on the subject if I were you."

"He knows my views on marriage."

"I doubt he thought of that conversation once since. Now, I think that is all my duty to you ever required. Until we meet again, Lord Raphael, Claymore." Ian glanced hard at Jimmy where he blocked the exit and after a moment of hesitation, James stepped aside so he could leave.

When the door was closed, Rafe righted the hall bench, sat down and put his head into his hands. He would not put it past his father to carry out what Ian suggested and arrange a marriage for him. Norwich would scheme until he had his way and a duke with an heiress as a ward would be temptation enough to make him the most agreeable guest the Duke of Staines had likely ever had.

The one thing in his favor was that the duke knew Rafe's tastes did not include bedding women and was sure to find a way around such a match.

James settled at his side and placed one arm around his back. Rafe leaned into his friend and thanked heaven again for bringing them together at such a time. He placed a hand on James's thigh. "Ian did not act as if he wished me harm."

"I agree. He's irritating, but the hurt he displayed at the accusations seemed very real. He loves Norwich and has always tried to please him. It's painful to watch at times."

Norwich *did* treat his sons differently and as much as Rafe didn't like it he had no power to change their father's behavior. Ian tried to make their father see him and be proud of his achievements while Rafe tried to avoid Norwich as much as possible. One day, Ian would become the Earl of Norwich, after Rafe died childless and of old age. He comforted himself with the knowledge. It was the way it had to be but he couldn't very well inform Ian of the reason marriage was so abhorrent to him. He would make it up to him somehow but not today.

Today, he had a wedding to derail before it was too late. "We should go see my father."

CHAPTER FOURTEEN

The duke's smartly dressed footman gestured to the door behind him. "Your father will see you now, Lord Raphael."

Since Rafe had been kept waiting an anxious quarter-hour while he was told his father was being made presentable for company, he hurried into the guest bedchamber in the Duke of Staines residence to find his father still on the bed, but dressed now and with a breakfast tray beside him. He looked up guiltily as he set aside what appeared to be a half-empty bowl of pudding. "Not a word to your mother," he cautioned.

He counted the empty bowls on the tray. Nine stacked untidily and all surprisingly clean. "No, not a word to mine," Rafe replied. His mother was dead. He'd never considered his father's second wife in any way motherly toward him and certainly not now there was a possibility she might have tried to kill them both so her son might advance to the title of earl. "You look well."

His father took one last suck on the spoon and dropped it to the tray. "We should talk."

Rafe glanced behind him. James had not followed him inside. He lingered some distance away in the hallway beyond, out of his father's line of sight. Since James had no better chance at persuading Norwich, Rafe knew he was on his own. "About?"

"I think you know. Shut the door."

He sighed and did as he bid, although he'd rather not hear his father was scheming with the Duke of Staines or planning to. He crossed the room and stood alert beside the bed though ready to run. From years of experience, he'd learned not to prompt these sudden confidential conversations. The end result was always the same whether he initiated the conversation or waited Norwich out. He generally found no joy in them.

"What mood holds sway over Claymore these days?"

"Claymore?" Rafe couldn't hide the surprise he felt at having his friend brought into the conversation.

"Yes. Yes." His father lowered his voice to a surprisingly gentle tone. "You clearly are still on friendly terms. I thought perhaps you'd fallen out of favor with the gentleman."

"No. We are still the best of friends." Rafe's skin began to crawl. "The same as we've ever been."

"Good. Good." His father cast a lingering look at the discarded tray as if he were still hungry. "I need you to stay on his good side. Butter him up. Make him feel important. Part of the family as it were."

"And why would I need to do that?"

His father's nose wrinkled with distaste. "Obvious."

"No, Father. It really is not."

His father sighed, a long slow breath that made his nostrils flare and his chest deflate dramatically. It was the same false display of emotion he'd employed to get his way, right before he began to yell and bluster. The action alerted Rafe to the fact that his father's health *was* much improved and that made him quite dangerous. His next words were always the most important. "There is a match to be made if we are quick and decisive."

"A match?" Pretending ignorance would slow him down. "With whom?"

His father waved his hand toward the door. "Claymore's sister is of age."

Rafe could feel his eyes widening in shock despite his plans to remain unruffled. "She's like a sister to me."

"Brotherly feelings go a long way to smoothing things over in cases such as these. Despite the unpleasantness of our health, I'd like this settled before the week is out."

"No. Absolutely not." He swallowed hard. "I'm not marrying Caitlin."

His father shook his head. "I was not talking about you. I want her for Ian. Damn fool's besotted."

Rafe didn't believe that for a moment. Ian and Caitlin had met only a handful of times. There had to be a mistake. "For Ian? Did the poison corrupt your mind as well as your appetite? That's a terrible suggestion. I'll make sure it doesn't happen."

His father held up his hands for peace. "Keep your voice down. Are you always so excitable? Marrying your brother to Claymore's sister will solve everything."

So it wasn't a match for him but for his brother that Norwich was planning. Never trust him to be in anyway direct. "And the fact that someone tried to poison the pair of us isn't of interest to you."

His father shifted uncomfortably in his bed, but he said nothing, his lips clamped shut in a hardline.

"You do know I have formed my own suspicions as to who might have the most to gain if both of us were to perish. That would be Ian, in case your mind is so full of making dynastic matches that you cannot see the immediate problem."

"The matter will be dealt with."

"Before or after they succeed in causing our hearts to stop?"

"You are not in any danger if you keep to your usual habits."

"My habits."

"Breakfast with me and your remaining meals elsewhere."

"But it is at breakfast that the poisoning occurred." He couldn't believe this. "I cast up my accounts after eating the remainder of your breakfast just once. I have never felt so ill."

His father's cheeks flamed. "Do you expect an apology that I chose my second wife so poorly?"

Rafe drew back his head as if he had been struck. "She's trying to kill you."

His father sighed heavily, looking every bit his fifty-nine years. "You are safe from harm if you remain Claymore's guest and I urge you to make the most of the opportunity for your brother's sake. I frank so much correspondence to Claymore's estate than ever and it's not all written to him."

"Ian writes to Caitlin? I don't believe that."

"It is the truth whether you choose to believe me or

not. Now do be good and let me see Claymore. Mustn't keep him waiting any longer."

His father smiled and although Rafe wanted nothing more than to pretend this was not happening, he stood and opened the door to James, ushering him into the sick room.

"Claymore," his father greeted James expansively, his grin wide and welcoming.

James leaned across the bed to shake hands and then drew back. "I trust you're health has improved, my lord."

"Indeed it has. Indeed it has. As fit as an ox," Norwich boasted, thumping his chest. "The duke sets a good table, even when it's held over one's lap. Just as you do for my son there. He was just telling me how fine a host you've been to him and I do thank you for taking such good care of him."

"Of course." A frown line appeared between James' eyebrows as he no doubt grew suspicious of Norwich's hearty friendliness. "I believe him almost completely recovered. His appetite has returned as it appears your has."

His father laughed and patted his stomach fondly. "How long are you staying in London and when does your family join you? It's been an age since your mother and I have talked."

CHAPTER FIFTEEN

James answered the Duke of Staines urgent summons and presented himself at Staine's townhouse promptly at three o'clock. The servant that bid him enter and took his hat and gloves said not a word so he was surprised to find a large gathering in the library he was shown to. Only a few faces were unfamiliar. The Duke of Staines was flanked by his younger brother--a cheerful clergyman he'd seen about St. Georges Church on several occasions. The dukes of Byworth and Armitage had chairs to one side of the room. Lord and Lady Norwich sat together with his sons, Rafe and Ian, behind them. But the three other gentlemen in the room were very much a mystery to him. They appeared quite bookish and severe. They didn't speak to anyone.

The doors closed behind his back and when James turned to look who'd joined them last he smiled. Redding, the duke's man, took a place before the doors as if standing sentry.

The Duke of Staines stood and addressed the room. "The punishment for murder is death by hanging. Attempted murder garners the same punishment no matter that a death hasn't occurred."

Every eye focused on the duke. He commanded the room and everyone in it.

"Have you ever witnessed a hanging? Have you ever witnessed the death of one whom you might not be sure to be guilty of the crime he was convicted for?"

A few voices murmured yes. Most in the room bowed their heads.

"An unfortunate situation has arisen. One that gives me great pain because suspecting one of blame is logical, yet not entirely so. I have summoned you all here, my trusted friends, to help me decide what to do. Our laws dictate that a magistrate should be involved. The criminal brought to judgment before the public and held up for the ridicule they deserve."

A mutter rose around the room and the duke held up his hands for silence.

"An attempt has been made on the life of the Earl of Norwich this past week. A vicious poisoner attempted to slowly sicken him in a way designed to avoid immediate suspicion. I am informed by many learned physicians that the dose must have been precisely doled out to avoid a sudden death in the victim. In this case, the poisoner was thwarted by Lord Raphael. If not for his abundant appetite and compassion, dispersing the poison to a younger man and stronger constitution, then Norwich would surely be dead today."

Those who'd not seemed interested suddenly stood and drew closer to Norwich.

The duke prowled the room, pausing to occasionally nod to those gathered about him. "My friends, I invited you here today not to accuse but to decide what should be done to prevent such unpleasant events from happening again."

The duke studied Norwich a long moment, mostly James suspected for dramatic effect. "Norwich has two sons. Lord Raphael, as I've explained, has suffered from the poisoning too and has fled the family home to recuperate. That leaves Lord Ian, a spare to be sure but one whose health is, by all accounts, sound. So far, he's not come to the poisoner's attention and I hope that day never arrives." The Duke of Staines paused beside James. "Do you know that women are spared a public hanging if convicted of murder?"

He glanced at Ian and saw his face whiten. "They are burned alive at the stake, are they not?"

Ian darted a glance to his own mother. His jaw clenched tight before he lowered his gaze to the floor.

The duke continued. "Sometimes, they are smothered first before the flames take them. It is a small mercy."

To James' surprise, Rafe put a comforting hand on his brother's shoulder. They looked at each other and Ian shuddered so violently that James crossed the room. The young man must suspect his mother had a hand in the poisoning. Of anyone, he probably knew her ambitions.

On the chaise lounge before them, Norwich and his second wife said not a word nor did they look at each other. There was no show of concern from Lady Norwich for the threat against her husband and stepson. She said not one word on the subject and that confirmed for James that however the actual poisoning had occurred, she wasn't the least bit concerned about the prospect of being a widow or the mother of one less son.

"I would like to visit the sea coast if I may father," Ian said suddenly.

Norwich turned slowly, blinking up at his youngest son. "No."

Ian swallowed. "The expense will be minimal. I'll take just one servant and live very simply."

"You'll do no such thing." Lady Norwich burst out. "You've done nothing wrong."

Ian stared at his mother. "I cannot live in London with everyone thinking my behavior is suspect in poisoning my father and brother. I have the most to gain should they die. No one will believe in my innocence. I cannot live like this and I won't."

"No one is accusing anyone, Lord Ian," Staines quickly cut in. "This gathering is merely to prevent further mischief. Each gentleman present will keep the matter private, I swear, so long as Norwich and Raphael remain in perfectly natural good health. I would not like to hear of further sickness inflicted upon them. Do I make myself very clear? The consequences for the title could be disastrous."

"For the title?" The countess queried.

"Well, yes. I imagine the King would look unfavorably upon a succession begun in suspicious circumstances. The title, lands and wealth of the family involved could be stripped away leaving them less than penniless beggars on a street corner."

James glanced down in time to see the countess shudder. She glanced sideways for a split second then licked her lips. "I'm sure Norwich will be himself directly."

"Good, good."

Redding chose that moment to crack the doors wide and those assembled ambled out after wishing Norwich and Rafe a speedy recovery.

Norwich hefted himself from the chair with a groan and shuffled across the room, choosing to sit again far away from his wife. Redding handed him a whiskey and tucked a footstool under his feet.

Ian broke away, rounded the chaise and knelt before his mother. "Mother."

James caught Rafe's arm and dragged him out of earshot. "We don't need the confirmation, do we?"

"Certainly not." Rafe muttered, his chest rising and falling.

He blocked his friend's view of Ian and Lady Norwich by standing directly before Rafe. "Are you well enough to go boating today?"

"Today?" Rafe shook his head. "Not today. I feel sick over this."

Although it was unwise given Norwich's presence, James rubbed up and down Rafe's arm to soothe him. "Dinner and then bed?"

"Bed sounds very nice." Rafe sighed and the beginnings of a smile appeared. "As long as you are there with me," he whispered.

His heart swelled with peace and hope. He'd feared how the culprit of the poisoning would be identified and brought to justice, but it seemed the duke has less love for the public spectacle of hangings than he did. If only the room weren't so crowded he'd take Rafe into his arms and hold him like that forever.

But forever had to wait a bit longer. When they returned to Claymore house, he'd hold Rafe and a whole lot more all night long.

CHAPTER SIXTEEN

Rafe had just closed the door behind him when the shrill demand from a feminine voice cut through his budding lust like the sharpest blade.

"Where have you been?"

He spun about to find a pair of delicate arms wrapped around his lover. Claymore sputtered a bit and then set his sister Caitlin at arm's length. "What the devil are you doing here?"

Caitlin, small and dainty but with a determination to match her brother, merely smiled and ignored the hostility in James' voice. "Is that any way to welcome your sister on her first trip to London?"

"And it may well be your last. You are supposed to be at Claymore. Where is Mama?"

She smiled at Rafe and held out her hand. "Lord Raphael! What a pleasure to see you again."

"Lady Caitlin. The pleasure is mine." Rafe took her hand and squeezed, but then Caitlin surprised him by looping her arm through his and leading him into the imperfectly uncovered drawing room.

She looked about her with a frown. "How is your father faring now?"

"How do you know about that?"

She winced. "I cannot confess my source, but I hope the worst hasn't come to pass."

Ian has confided in her. "My father is well."

James stalked out of the room and thundered up the staircase.

Caitlin let out a long breath. "That is a relief. I've been so concerned. I do hope I have the chance to call on your father soon. I had thought to wait till Claymore obliged and escorted me. However, given the news he is on the mend perhaps merely passing on my best wishes and hopes for a speedy recovery will be enough."

"I certainly shall when I see him. It won't be until tomorrow morning at breakfast."

Caitlin's face fell. "Oh, well another day it must be."

He settled her on the uncovered chaise and flicked off another cover on a straight-backed chair for himself. "How have you been?"

"Oh, I'm always well. I must say I am more glad to see you here with my brother than I can possibly relate."

"Oh. Why is that?"

She glanced quickly at the doorway. "In truth, I'm not as concerned for your father as I am for James. Does he seem... like his old self to you?"

"Yes." Rafe shrugged rather than answer honestly. "Your brother never changes," he lied easily to spare her pain. Caitlin had always been too perceptive for her own good.

"It's just that..." Her voice trailed off as James stormed into the room.

"Where is Mama, Caitlin, and no avoiding the question this time?"

She stared at him defiantly. "Mama is at Claymore."

"And how did you get to London."

"On the stage. It really is quite an efficient means of transport."

"On the stage?" Rafe quickly stood. "Do you have any idea how dangerous this is?"

She swiftly glanced between them. "I believe less so than being spoken down to by the pair of you as if I were a child."

"You are a child. A silly fool." James raked a hand through his hair. "Mama will be out of her mind with fear by now. How could you do this to her?"

"I left a note behind," Caitlin informed them smugly. "I told her I was coming straight here to see you and that she should trust me."

James growled, and not the way that excited Rafe. He stormed from the room again and Rafe could hear him in the next room opening drawers and slamming them closed again. He stared at Caitlin and saw satisfaction on her face. "That was not well done of you," he chided.

She sat primly again, her face serene. "I would not need to resort to drastic measures to garner a little attention from him. He acts as if we are worlds apart, but I need him to care about me."

"He does care for you. More than you will ever know. No one likes to have their heart stopped by fear for a loved one."

"Do you even know what he's been doing these last months?" She shook her head enough that the pretty ringlets on each side jiggled. "He's moody and surly, I cannot get him to sit still long enough to discuss my coming out. My friends are all here for the Season or planning their come outs for next year, but not me. Oh no. I can wait, he said."

Rafe sympathized with Caitlin, but he alone knew why James had refused to make any plans beyond his birthday. He'd planned to be dead when his sister made her come out, six months to a year depending on how long she mourned. "Be patient with him."

Caitlin narrowed her eyes. "Do you not think it strange he refuses to even order a new coat? I fear the worst."

From the corner of his eye he saw James approach the door and stop. "What did you imagine?"

"Is it true our pockets are to let?" Caitlin slipped off her shoes and curled up against the arm of the chaise like a lost little girl, eyes wide with worry. "He could have simply told me the truth. I would understand. Papa made a mess of everything."

"It's not that," James said as he hurried to her side. When he drew her into his arms, Rafe added another item to his list of reasons why he loved the man. He had the greatest heart. "I had some thinking to do about my life, but that's in the past now and there is nothing to worry about."

Caitlin curled against him. "You could have talked to me."

"I know." James glanced up at Rafe and the guilt in his eyes tore at him.

He smiled softly, knowing there wasn't anything else he could do but love the man and offer silent support from afar. He stood and strolled from the room, giving them a few moment's privacy.

As he entered the dining room he realized that any plans they may have wanted to make for pleasure were at an end for now. With Caitlin here, he probably shouldn't even stay the night. There wasn't a chaperone present and despite thinking of her as a sister, Society would talk before she even made her come out.

He turned on his heel to return to James and found him and his sister standing directly in his path. "Caitlin wishes to visit a neighbor who lives nearby and has a daughter her age. I thought perhaps since Mama isn't here and there are no servants or even a chaperone about the place that she would do better there overnight until I can make other plans."

"Of course."

"I will be back soon, I promise. Their townhouse is just two streets away." James appeared ready to say more, but with his sister smiling at them he likely didn't dare.

"Very well."

They left then, and Rafe watched them go as far as he was able. When they were out of sight he hurried upstairs, found a vacant room and made it look as if he'd been sleeping there all along instead of in James' bed.

CHAPTER SEVENTEEN

Sisters were a complication James hadn't needed or imagined he'd have to deal with yet. As he let himself into his bedroom, his mind was filled with worry over what she'd concluded about the state of his bed. Rumpled and sleep tossed with two pillows bearing the impression of two heads. Signs of a wild night of unbridled sex, clothes strewn about but not a woman's garment in sight.

Since he didn't see Rafe about, he called out his name.

"In here," Rafe replied, his voice muffled as if coming from a distance away.

James followed the sound, surprised to find Rafe reclining on another bed. The man appeared to be waking from sleep. He strolled in, eyeing the room that now exuded a lived-in feel that had been absent before. Beside the bed there was an open book, a bottle of wine along with a half-full glass. In his absence, Rafe had moved into another room and James regretted that it must be so.

"Good evening."

Rafe glanced at the door. "Hmm, sorry. Must have dozed off. What time is it?"

"Quite a bit later than I expected to be. The Argyle's like to talk and I couldn't just dump my sister and run."

"No. That might be noticed." Rafe stretched and then sat up slowly. "I gather everything is settled for her stay."

He nodded. "She's had her ears scolded severely by Lady Argyle who is a great friend to my mother and insisted a servant be dispatched to Claymore with the news Caitlin is safe and well. She will remain there until Mama arrives in Town."

"Ah, your mother is coming."

"It is inevitable." Jimmy leaned against the bedpost. "What shall we do with our night?"

Rafe grinned wickedly. "I can think of any number of

pleasant activities, but there is an unpleasant one we should talk about now."

"Your father's plans for marriage." When Rafe nodded, he sat beside him.

"Who did he have in mind?"

"You won't believe it, but he means to make a match with your sister."

"Mine." Jimmy sprang up from the bed. "Oh, no."

Rafe began to chuckle. "That was almost exactly my reaction. Thankfully he didn't mean for me to marry her. He has this insane notion in his head that Caitlin and Ian should make a match. Honestly, I cannot think of anyone worse for her."

James wasn't so sure he agreed. "You do know they write to each other, don't you?"

"Yes, my father told me." Rafe looked at him curiously. "Why didn't you?"

"Never gave it too much thought. Do you remember when Caitlin was fourteen and some local girls were treating her poorly? Ian, I believe, played a part in giving her the courage to stand up to them. They've corresponded since then. I had thought it merely a friendship. Perhaps it's not."

Rafe groaned. "She would make an excellent countess, despite the burden of marrying my brother."

"I should think so," James agreed. He'd spent a fortune on her education and he'd rather see that knowledge and poise put to good use. "I wanted her to marry into a family I respected, so..."

"Except for my stepmama's homicidal tendencies you'd support the marriage."

"If there was love." He nodded. "She'd have to love him and he her."

"Now that I don't have the faintest idea about." Rafe rolled to his feet. "Ian does not confide in me and up 'till now I've been quite content with that. I suppose if the idea has any merit we'll have to determine their feelings."

"It's not as if they have to marry straightaway," James added, aware he was presuming to make plans for Caitlin without consulting her first or allowing her the benefit of a first Season. He was merely talking over the matter with his friend. But he could see the possibilities clearly. Binding the two families together in such a way made mutual visits and gatherings even easier, as long as Lady Norwich remained out of their lives.

"No, but if they don't think of each other in those terms Norwich may still try to match them. I wouldn't like Ian to compromise Caitlin because of his scheming."

"We will put a stop to any of that."

"We certainly will." Rafe crossed back to James, leaned down and parted his thighs. He stepped into the gap between and looped his arms around his neck. "But first a kiss before we hide the fact we can barely keep our hands off each other."

"That's going to be hard."

Rafe rubbed the heel of his hand over James' groin. "As you are right now."

He sagged back against the mattress to give Rafe access to the fastenings of his trousers. His cock sprang free soon after and he was rewarded with the warmth of Rafe's mouth surrounding him. He slowly thrust his hips into that warmth, letting himself fall into their lovemaking as if it wasn't still a revelation to him. He groaned when Rafe's hands slipped low to knead his arse.

Rafe slowly shifted his fingers until they traced the crack of his arse. He widened James' legs a little more, tilting his hips too. A fingertip brushed against his hole and James jerked away, surprised by the new sensation.

His lover did not pause or apologize for the shock he'd delivered. He sucked James' cock so thoroughly that when his fingers drifted there again the next touch was wanted. His cock throbbed as those light touches grew more insistent. Rafe pulled off his cock to wet his finger, then returned to tormenting James' arse.

When he pushed in, James was ready but not for the burst of lust that filled his whole body. He shoved his cock hard into Rafe's mouth as he in turn was breached. His arse burned, his breathing hitched. He reached for his lover as his world shrank to what pleasure his friend offered with so little effort.

Rafe lifted his head. "Oil me. It's beneath the pillow."

He held out one hand, fingers curled over his palm to form a cup. James, on the verge of spilling his seed, was glad of the distraction. A practical chore was just the thing to hold his release at bay a little longer. He concentrated on coating Rafe's fingers, and when he was done finally met his friend's merry gaze. "You're loving this," he said softly. "You'll like the rest even more."

Rafe braced his arm against the back of James' legs and rolled him slightly so his arse was even more exposed. The touch against his hole returned. A small flicker of pain, followed by a feeling of violation. James strove to keep his breathing calm. When Rafe began to fuck him with a finger, his seed shot over his belly before he could stop it.

His lover paused as he finished, his eyes glowing with mirth. "That was quick."

"Oh shut up."

Rafe laughed and returned his attention to James' arse. "One day I'm going to have my cock here and you, sir, are going to scream like that all over again."

"I did not scream."

"You most certainly did. It's a good thing you do not have any servants at present. They'd think I was murdering you instead of making you very, very happy." Rafe rimmed his opening a few more times. Just when James thought that was all he'd do the man pressed his finger inside, fucking him with it. He paused again and this time he winced at the pain.

"That's two." Rafe's voice had dropped to a deep growl and James found the unusual timbre arousing enough that his cock tingled. Rafe worked his arse so thoroughly he was sure he could come again and soon.

Given the position he was currently in, bent over himself, arse spit on Rafe's fingers, he couldn't touch Rafe at all to bring him the same relief. And he wanted to be fair, very much. He'd like to do the same to his lover. He grabbed the flask of oil and dribbled some on his fingers. "My turn."

Rafe chuckled. "I'm surprised you waited this long to try to take over. Scoot down the bed. We can pleasure each other this way at the same time."

James wasn't sure what Rafe meant until he climbed on top with his cock and balls dangling in James face. He wriggled around to free his arms and found Rafe's arse soon enough. He slid his finger inside the tight passage at the same time as Rafe.

It wasn't the same as fucking, but his lover moaned and pushed back into him. Very soon he decided that one finger was simply not enough. He added another and then reconsidered. Rafe could take his cock very easily. He added a third and the body hovering above him shuddered.

James glanced along the slender length poised above him and saw a neglected cock with seed dripping from the tip. He shifted to grasp it and drew it back toward his mouth. With a bit of maneuvering, he managed to taste just the head before Rafe swore and filled his mouth with his seed.

The spasms went on forever, or so it seemed to James. Rafe squeezed tightly around his fingers and he slowly withdrew them until his hand was free. When Rafe finished, he slumped to his side. "Damn fast learner."

His hard cock didn't like being abandoned so he moved over Rafe where he'd fallen and brushed the hard length against his thigh. "Is that a complaint?"

"Oh, no." Rafe scrambled for the oil again and coated James's cock. "It's a trait I admire along with your flattering desire to have me again." He pulled his upper leg toward his chest and James positioned himself at a slightly different angle.

He slid inside with a groan, worked himself as deeply as he could and then held still above Rafe, admiring how effortlessly they came together. "You'd tell me if I wanted it too much wouldn't you?"

"You haven't reached my limit yet." He awkwardly rolled onto his belly then brought himself up to his knees while James was still lodged in him. He pressed his face against the bedding, turned slightly so James could see his profile. He closed his eyes and then he did the most arousing thing of his life. He placed his hands across his back, crossed at the wrists.

The posture was one of submission. Of complete and utter trust. James' cock almost burst with need as he captured Rafe's wrists and held them. He started to move, making love to Rafe slowly, deeply. Long firm thrusts that forced him to moan in time with them. James stared at what he did. Seeing his cock sink into Rafe again and again, swelling impossibly with each thrust and groan brought him peace and power and filled his soul.

He released Rafe's hands and caught his hips instead. He squeezed as he pounded an arse that seemed made just for him. He couldn't stop, couldn't hold back even if he tried. Rafe's hands disappeared beneath him and a touch ghosted over his balls. "Sneaky," he grunted out, slamming into Rafe as the man bucked and spilled his seed again.

James fell forward as his own release shot deep. His world turned over and when he came to rest he was right were he was supposed to be. Held tight in Rafe's arms. The only man in the world who truly did understand who he was and what he wanted.

EPILOGUE

One Week Later

Everyone delighted that the Earl of Claymore was once more a figure in Society, especially the husband hunting debutantes and lonely widows who thought to tempt him to their beds. Rafe gritted his teeth and James waltzed by with yet another woman in his arms. It had been a week since his last night in Jimmy's bed and he still didn't know if there would be another. Their last tryst had been intense, sensual and above all else fun. After the first pleasure, they had talked, wrestled and loved each other with their mouths. Sex had never been so enjoyable before and Rafe knew the reason why.

He'd never truly made love before.

When he left James' bed he never looked at himself in the mirror later with any doubts lingering in the back of his mind. He loved James so completely, so naturally, that he had no room for guilt. Their connection made his life worthwhile, complete, in a way it never had before.

When morning had brightened the sky beyond James' windows, Rafe had slipped from his bed without a word about their future and returned to the Duke of Staines home to share breakfast with his father. Despite the vigorous lovemaking, he'd walked home with more energy than he could ever remember, absolutely sure that their next romantic encounter would be soon and just as thrilling.

Yet that brief anticipation hadn't lasted beyond two days. James, already distracted by his sister's sudden arrival, had gained his mother's company too, and the need to hire staff for his London townhouse again took precedence on his time. Rafe had only seen him in the company of others. They never had a chance to arrange to meet again, and Rafe was becoming increasingly concerned he might have expected more than James was able to give.

The dance ended and James led his partner from the floor in the direction opposite of where Rafe stood. When he began a conversation with the chit's father with no appearance of ending it soon, Rafe shook his head in disgust. He'd been a fool to imagine a settled life with Jimmy that would not include ladies.

He lowered his eyes to hide his disappointment. His love for James might be the single-most important event of his life, but it was not something he could show openly. He'd been completely honest and open to James. Yet he had not told James that he was truly loved. He'd lost the chance and couldn't see how he'd claim another. Not with every ear in Society paused to watch for the next indiscretion.

Rafe prowled the ballroom of Slater House, determined not to spend yet another night mooning over his lover. It was hard to forget he now knew James in intimate detail. The weight of his balls, the taste of his seed, the sound of him moaning his ecstasy at the moment of release. Frustration coursed through him, and he turned away. He was being as ridiculous as any young woman smitten by an unattainable man.

There was no point remaining. James would be occupied all night, watching over his sister as she took her first steps into Society. Since he had no further need to dance with Caitlin tonight, he need not remain and torture himself.

Rafe collected his top hat and gloves. He stepped out onto the street and looked left and right. It was too early to go home and his father's recent brush with mortality made him uncomfortably sentimental. Normally, it wouldn't bother him overmuch except his father had taken to mentioning James, and his hopes for the marriage between Ian and Caitlin every chance he got.

He hailed a hack, gave directions to the Hunt Club, and climbed inside. As he pulled the door closed, it was ripped from his grip. To his surprise, Jimmy climbed inside and sat on the opposite seat. "Where the hell are you going?"

"The Hunt Club. What's it to you?"

His lover sat forward, hands sliding over Rafe's thighs. "I wanted to see you."

"You were occupied."

A frown grew on James' face and he looked away. The truth was that he was jealous that debutantes could touch his lover in public. The most Rafe had managed was to shake James' hand each night. The touch was far too brief to bring any satisfaction.

"Mama wanted to make an early exit to entice suitors into visiting tomorrow, she said." James fell to his knees between the carriage seats. "I don't know how to do this."

Rafe eyed him warily. "Do what?"

"Love you." Jimmy's chest rose as he took a deep breath. "I have no clue how to proceed."

Rafe gaped. "You love me?"

"Of course." He shifted to sit at Rafe's side. "I've known you all my life. You're my best friend. You let me . . ." James' smile grew shy. "You gave me the best nights of my life and I'm damned if I can work out how to have that and you with me while we are in Town."

Rafe's heart and thoughts tumbled over themselves in a rush of wonder and hope. "I thought you'd had enough of me."

James caught his chin and lifted his face to his. "Can't stop thinking about how damn lucky I am to have you in my life."

When he kissed him gently, Rafe draped his arms about his broad shoulders and pulled him closer. It was risky to kiss in the semi-privacy of a dark carriage with the curtains undrawn, but he hoped it was dark enough that no one would recognize them should they look in.

With a heavy sigh, James drew back. "You have the sweetest lips."

Rafe grinned. "And you have the sweetest cock."

A rumbling laugh left James. "Your tight arse trumps everything."

He drew back as they both burst out laughing. His uncertainly disappeared as James pressed close. He pulled him into his embrace again and squeezed. "What do we do now?"

"I imagine we find a nice quiet place and make love."

"Can't go home. My mother and sister have settled in for what remains of the Season." James' frown grew. "I don't mean just for tonight. I mean forever after that."

Rafe frowned too. "I don't know. I've never had a lover who is also my friend."

"You'd better get used to it," James growled. "Seriously, how can we manage this without detection? Our homes are occupied. I want to see you in London, especially without your clothes on."

He slumped in his seat. "Well, that rules out tonight."

James laid a hand over Rafe's groin and rubbed. "Not necessarily."

Rafe groaned as his cock thickened. "We'll be at the Hunt Club soon."

James knocked on the roof and gave the driver new directions.

"Where are we going?"

James pressed harder against Rafe's erection. "I'd almost forgotten. My father had a mistress in London. I sent her packing long ago, but I still have the house. We are going there so we can talk this out properly."

"Just talk?"

"Well, no. I had a little more than talking in mind." James' touch firmed causing Rafe to wish they could continue in the carriage. But that too was risky. He couldn't place James' life and reputation in jeopardy. Instead, he pushed James' hand away and thought about debutants. His ardor cooled quickly.

By the time the carriage came to a stop, Rafe had his body under control. James stepped out first, paid the driver, and ushered Rafe into the dark house. Once inside and the door closed, he hauled him close and kissed him soundly. "I've been waiting all week to do that. Come upstairs."

When James lit a candle, Rafe looked about, liking what he saw at first glance very much. "Not yet," he whispered. He took the candle and prowled the lower floor; parlor, study, dining room and small empty kitchen at the back. A narrow staircase ascended to an upper floor. James waited on the third step. When Rafe joined him, his lover caught his hand and together they started up the stairs.

They both jumped as a heavy knock sounded on the door behind them. They looked at each other and then James strode downward and wrenched the front door open.

Mr. Redding stood on the uppermost step. The man didn't smile as he thrust out a letter. "His Grace sent this with his compliments."

"Thank you." James took the note and the next moment Redding was gone, back to a black carriage parked a short distance away.

James closed the door, eyeing the note with a puzzled frown. "What could the duke want with me at this hour?"

Rafe's heart raced with excitement. "Well, open it and find out or we will never know."

He broke the seal and read, taking a few steps away as he did so. "It's an invitation to dine with him."

Disappointment crashed through him. "When?"

"Tomorrow." James turned and he grinned. "What does one wear to one's first visit to the Hunt Club? Seems His Grace has decided he likes me."

Rafe wrapped his arms around James and squeezed him tightly. "That solves the problem of how we can be alone."

James frowned. "How so?"

"The Hunt Club is for pleasure. There are endless opportunities for sex behind those doors at any hour of the day and night."

The frown grew severe. "So, that is how you've managed your affairs. At a sex club?"

He nodded quickly, but was surprised James found offence in the idea. He would see for himself tomorrow that there was more to it than that. "I cannot wait to show you the club. All my life I've wanted you there with me."

"To watch you have sex with prostitutes?"

Rafe shook his head. "To have sex with you. The club caters to unique needs. A man may go there simply as he would go to White's, but if he's feeling amorous, he may find what he needs upstairs. There are men and women whose sole delight is to bring the member' pleasure. I have noticed other lords like us form closer bonds there too. We may sit side by side, hands on each other's thighs and no one will even blink. We take a vow, you see, to protect each other's reputations and in turn protect our own. We will be safe to love each other there when ever we want."

"So, everyone there would know about us?" James asked, his voice hesitant.

"Unless you prefer them not to."

James tapped the note against his palm. "I will have to think about it."

"Of course." Rafe hadn't considered James might find that aspect of the club distressing. He found it a relief to be around men who didn't judge or condemn him for his preferences. Perhaps it was too soon for James to see that side of the equation. "Not all members fully partake of the club's pleasure rooms. The chef is quite remarkable and I enjoy dining there when I need to."

His friend nodded and slipped the invitation to the table beside the door. Rafe caught his hand, aware James wouldn't rush to make a decision no matter how much he pushed or begged. He'd weigh up all the benefits and risks and decide what he could bear.

Rafe pulled him up the stairs and peeked into the bedrooms and closets, noting the furniture was first rate and the linen closet full. It wasn't a big house. It would suit one person or a newly married couple perfectly. An idea formed. If James did not accept the club membership they would still need somewhere to meet and this place could certainly do. "What will you do with this place?"

James scowled. "It's entailed, unfortunately, so I'm stuck with my father's love nest."

"Lease it to me." Rafe bit his lip after the impulsive demand slipped out. He could imagine living here, well away from his father's daily confidences and his brother's glum mood. He could have freedom and much needed privacy. He could have precious time alone with James and that was what mattered most.

If he hired only a few servants that came in during the mornings, no one would know what they did together after that.

James crowded him, his eyes assessing. "Why didn't I think of that?"

"Because you are not in daily proximity to my father." Rafe grinned. "It's time I found a place of my own and asserted my independence. It's not too big for me to afford."

"Especially if you don't marry for a while."

He scowled. "I have no intention of ever marrying. I'll happily leave my brother and his offspring the title."

James' expression grew pained. "I don't have a brother, but I do have a cousin who will inherit. I brought him up to Claymore last month."

Rafe tightened his grip on James. Before his friend had come to London he'd thought he couldn't live his life the way he wanted and he'd been prepared to give up everything, his very life, to save his family the shock of learning of his inclinations. "And now?"

"Once my sister is married and happily settled I'd thought of bringing him to visit Claymore more often. Let him get to know the place to see if he's a man of sense and if not I'll teach him what he needs to learn."

"You could marry if you wanted to," Rafe conceded, though he disliked the idea intensely. James was the type of man who took his responsibilities seriously. He would find a proper wife, marry to produce an heir for the estate, and guide that child toward his future very diligently. He'd hide his misery. Only Rafe would see it.

James firmly stroked down Rafe's back. "I don't want to think of it yet. Not tonight. Besides, we have the much more important task of seeing Caitlin married off well first, perhaps to your brother. That will take up quite a bit of time and energy."

Rafe nodded. "Then I'd better enjoy you while you have

the night free."

He smiled at James, seeing the topic troubled him more than he let on. There was nothing else that could be done tonight. Nothing else besides make each other as happy as possible in the short time they had like this. They might never be like other lords who revealed their lovers with few cares for the consequences. Hiding their affair and treasuring stolen moments would become their world. He squeezed Jimmy's hand and led him toward the room he'd decided to make his bedchamber when he moved in.

The room would be warm and sunny come morning. Perfect for rousing a sated man from a deep sleep in his lover's bed so he might slip home unnoticed.

In silence they stripped each other until they were equal and rubbed against each other's bare skin. James radiated such warmth and stared with such lust-filled eyes that Rafe scrambled on to the bed and held out both hands. "I used to dream of this moment, never thinking that such a wish could come true. I love you so much."

James smiled and Rafe's world shrank to this moment. "And I have always loved you. My friend. My confidant. Even if it was just a dream at first."

"Not just a dream now." He brushed their lips together. "A beautiful discovery. The best yet."

THE END

ABOUT THE AUTHOR

Bestselling historical author Heather Boyd believes every character she creates deserves their own happily-ever-after, no matter how much trouble she puts them through. With that goal in mind, she weaves sizzling English set love stories that push the boundaries of regency era propriety to keep readers enthralled until the wee hours of the morning. Brimming with new ideas, she frequently wishes she could type as fast as she conjures new storylines. While writing full time north of Sydney, Australia, Heather collects dust bunnies in all corners of the house and does her best to wrangle her testosterone-fuelled family into submission.

For more information visit
www.heather-boyd.com

ALSO BY HEATHER BOYD

The Distinguished Rogues Series:
Chills
Broken
Charity
An Accidental Affair
Keepsake
An Improper Proposal
Reason to Wed
The Trouble with Love
Married by Moonlight

The Wild Randalls Series:
Engaging the Enemy
Forsaking the Prize
Guarding the Spoils
Hunting the Hero

Miss Mayhem Series:
Miss Watson's First Scandal
Miss George's Second Chance
Miss Radley's Third Dare

Short Stories:
One Wicked Night
Wicked Mourning
In the Widow's Bed
Love Me Tender
Love Me True
The Almack's Alternative
A Husband for Mary

Book 1, Almost an Equal

When the Duke of Byworth's empty marriage is threatened by a fellow duke he is naturally aggrieved. Nathan cannot allow the potentially damaging contents of his wife's diary to reveal the depths of their estrangement because exposure of his secret dalliances with other men would taint his innocent children's lives. Not to mention end his life. So, without revealing his mission to his steward, Henry Stackpool, a man he trusts for everything else, Nathan undertakes to steal the diary back alone.

Former pickpocket and molly house whore, Henry Stackpool, works hard to keep his position as right hand to a moral man, the Duke of Byworth, but he fears his kind hearted employer is ill-equipped for a confrontation with his unstable opponent. Henry cannot explain the source of his knowledge without exposing the secrets of his past. So when fate places Henry in harm's way, he risks his hard won reputation and freedom to retrieve the duchess's diary himself.

Book 2, Barely a Master

The trappings of wealth and power give Aiden Banks, Duke of Lewes, little joy and certainly no pleasure. Tormented by grave mistakes he made in the past, he's learned control of his temper at great personal cost, finally shouldering the blame that he has lost the only man he had ever loved through his own actions. His only remaining goal is to educate his young heir to take his place as duke and then he will be free of his responsibilities.

Terrance Bridgewater has freedom at long last with no one to slow down his pursuit of reckless adventure. In London briefly en route to a ship bound for the continent, brings him face to face with his past. Running into the dark and dangerous Duke of Lewes is a complication he'd hoped to avoid. Despite his mistrust, the volatile duke's plea for a second chance tempts Terrance to lower his guard but on his terms only. Yet what can come of two souls with nothing in common but lies, opposing desires, and with far different futures ahead?

The Duke of Staines has the worst luck in wives and lovers. A widow for fifteen years, Ambrose is busy running his gentleman's club, snatches pleasure from transient lovers, and relies on Francis Redding to provide intelligent companionship between social engagements. There is only one problem with his relationship with Redding; the man would make the perfect lover, if only he wasn't a dependant servant.

Life-long footman to the Duke of Staines, Francis Redding, is hardly a stranger to the disappointment of unreachable dreams or the duke's unorthodox love life. He's lived in the duke's shadow for most of his life, trained as a surgeon at his request, too, and has all too frequently kept the duke out of trouble. It's not a bad life for a farmer's son, until the duke's luck runs out.

Victor Knight has never been able to juggle his work and love life to anyone's satisfaction. A hardworking investment banker in London, he's obsessed with maintaining his clients' privacy and profits, and cannot understand why those same clients are withdrawing funds when he's making them a good profit. When a dull evening supper at the Hunt Club ends in a blunt invitation to have sex with the Earl of Beecroft, he welcomes the distraction on the proviso they never discuss his business affairs.

Daniel Wellham, the Earl of Beecroft, has long admired Victor Knight. He even understands and admires the banker's preoccupation with work. Their night together is everything he hoped it would be and while he longs for permanence, his secret life as a spy means he can never reveal too much of his own history. Unfortunately, when he realizes that all is not right in Victor's life, those promises he made to keep his nose out of the banker's business means he cannot offer to help or explain that his latest mission might take him away forever. How can love and trust be possible when duty and responsibility prevent total honesty?